Scottish born, avid reader and alternate history buff, William C. Young now lives in Perth, Australia, enjoying the sunshine.

To my long-gone parents, wish you could see this.

William C. Young

PARVON ZIN
KOBAN HUNTER

AUSTIN MACAULEY PUBLISHERS™

LONDON • CAMBRIDGE • NEW YORK • SHARJAH

A CIP catalogue record for this title is available from the British Library.

ISBN 9781398476271 Paperback
ISBN 9781398476288 ePub e-book

www.austinmacauley.com

First Published 2023
Austin Macauley Publishers Ltd®
1 Canada Square
Canary Wharf
London
E14 5AA

Thanks to Austin Macauley Publishers for giving me a chance to let Zin and Co. see the light of day.

Table of Contents

New York May 1980

Zin looks in the hall mirror of his apartment in Hell's Kitchen New York, it is not that he dislikes what he is seeing, he has used this form for years. Too many in fact. He will need to move on soon, the old lady across the hall is starting to notice that he does not age. He shimmers, it's as if he is melting. Scales form as he morphs into his original Randorian form. It takes thirty seconds.

"That's better scalescrubber, I really don't like you being in human form."

"I know Ohna, it's why I change, to stop you nagging me."

"I am still your mate after all, it's not my fault that I died."

Zin shudders as the memory of that day flashes across his mind.

"I am glad I got you into the trans essence unit in time. Being alone on this backwater planet would have been the end of me. There is no way I would have survived against the Koban without you."

"True, remember to call in that last Koban contact."

"I will, though I do not think they are receiving us. We know the signal is being transmitted, but after all this time with no answer…What if the Koban destroyed Randor? What if the icing turned out to be permanent!”

"You can't think like that, now go call in."

“Your right Ohna. I will do it now.”

Zin walks over to his writing desk. In the bottom drawer is a flat metallic case, he lifts it out and breathes into a grill in its top, this disarms the security lock. He opens the hyper radio and starts his report.

“Parvon Zin calling from TXP73-S3. Koban contact report. Ohna and I tracked down a small clutch of Koban to a warehouse in lower Manhattan. Latitude 40.776676 Longitude -73.971321. Eight Koban have infiltrated a homeless shelter for humans, the bones found in the cellar of the building indicated they had been there for some time.”

Lower Manhattan one week ago.

Zin in the human form of Peter Randal gets a call from one of his network of human spies. She had tipped him off about strange happenings at a local homeless shelter. Zin uses down and outs and hookers as his eyes on the streets, he has been doing it for centuries. Sugar, a local prostitute witnessed two ‘monsters’ drag a homeless man into the basement of the shelter, curious she followed them, the screams from the basement made her blood run cold, the sight of two creatures devouring the poor man was horrifying. Remembering Zin paid good money for information about this kind of thing she called him straight away leaving a message on his answering machine.

Later that day Zin meets up with Sugar.

“Hi Peter, good to see you again. I am sure your creatures are in that building, what they did to that poor man was terrible.”

"Thanks Sugar, I will deal with it." Zin hands over fifty dollars and gets a kiss on the cheek as a thank you. Sugar disappears into the night. Zin starts his hunt.

Harrison Delgada or using his Koban identification 'smells stringent.' The Koban go by the unique smell of the individual, only using the human names when necessary. Harrison is the Alpha male of this all-male clutch, they had assimilated the original staff of the homeless shelter two years ago and now in typical Koban style were feasting off the poor souls in the shelter, they have killed and consumed hundreds of people, not one of them is missed or searched for.

The cunning Koban say the missing people have been sent to a better location as a reward, they actually have desperate people begging to be sent with them. The Koban happily oblige.

Zin watches the shelter from his car, out walks one of what he suspects is a Koban. Zin follows him. The man walks into a shadowed lane. Zin sneaks up behind him, a hand grasps the man's mouth. The small tendrils in Zin's palms enters the man's face, enzymes flow starting the assimilation process, this is when every shape shifter is defenceless as both bodies merge. It is thirty seconds before Zin has control of his new host body as memories and skills are transferred. This person was not a Koban. He was worse, he is a thrall. Humans who voluntarily serve the Koban. This piece of shit got to 'play' with the Koban's captives, the sociopathic madman did diabolical things to the poor people. Good enough. With this as swipe he has a way in, and now knows what the Koban's human bodies look like. All eight of them.

Harrison's memories are of the Koban being excited about an upcoming event. It seems someone's 'mother' was leaving town. All of the Koban were going to see her off. Zin has a bad feeling about that.

"Ohna, we may have one of the bangerups ready to leave the planet! According to this human they are going to Oregon."

"We will need to check it out scalecleaner, get some transport."

Zin hires a four-wheel drive and heads out towards Oregon. It is a four-day drive, with no need to sleep it's just a matter of fuel and food stops. As they enter Oregon Ohna starts to pick up Gravitox traces. They get stronger as they drive. Ohna unerringly guides Zin forward.

It is 8:32 am on the morning of May 1980.

Ohna screams, "Zin! the Gravitox readings are off the scale. Something is about to happen."

Directly in front of them is Mount St Helens.

The explosion rocks the car from side to side.

"Arrrg! We are too late. One of the scale-ticked parasites has matured enough to leave, by the size of that blast it was a smallish female. Just as well it was not like the original mother of these hells blasted bangerups. Remember the first one. The original mother of these scaleticks."

"Oh! I remember that all right, it was one of her brood that Killed me and our crewmates."

Team Oca, Twenty-Five Solar Cycles Since the Icing of Randor

Randor, now an icy ball still in the throes of an ongoing ice age brought on by the explosive blast of a super volcano that launched a Koban mother into space at great velocity. It was the vast amount of ash thrown into the atmosphere that cut out the sunlight bringing on the planet-wide ice age, millions die before the planet is fully evacuated.

Randorians

The Randorians like all shape shifting species do not sleep; their body recharges itself when inactive by simply staying still; their mitochondria vibrate maintaining energy levels in the cells; another body chemistry trait is their unusual DNA chain. Their 'telomeres' do not degrade through time, effectively all shapeshifters live forever. This does not happen of course, like all smallish animals they die for a variety of reasons, they are fairly frail in their natural form of a six to eight feet tall bipedal reptile, hence the survival tactic of subsuming a stronger host's body. The Randorians are the oldest of the shapeshifting species and have through the years fought their way to the top of the food chain, eliminating all the large carnivores on the planet, through superior intelligence and working in groups to defeat larger, stronger foes.

Now animal husbandry sees domesticated food animals raised and well cared for throughout their lives up until they are chosen for food, that is.

Then the instinctual 'Chase and Kill' eating frenzy occurs. Food chased down has more blood in its muscles, making it a far juicier meal, and eons old hunter instincts cannot be stopped. Special rooms in Randorian houses are designed to accommodate this act, plus outdoor eating areas are available for what would be the equivalent of a picnic. Hatchling Randorians start with the small chicken-sized 'Durgo' lizards and are taught the techniques in school of how to chase down and cleanly kill their food without injury to themselves; this is folded neatly into the school's meal breaktime.

The development of the Hyper Drive by the Randorians and the rise of the alliance of planets sees the Randorians as the alliances front line Koban Hunting element, the Koban being of such a threat to all, that the alliance jointly fund and train the hunter teams to locate and destroy the threat, the other members of the alliance provide tracking and early warning stations while the Randorians with their star drive are the only part of the alliance who are able to pursue the Koban pods. The Parvon, which is Randorian for hunter, are given the task.

The Parvon Teams are formed. Six highly trained Randorians form a hunter team. The Koban are such a threat an entire moon is put to use entirely for the Parvon. It houses its headquarters and living areas for its personnel and contains extensive training areas throughout the moons varied surface terrain from desert to lush forests.

The Randorians are also well known for their wicked sense of humour, and mating for life. The frills the females have on their head and down their neck cover all the colours of the rainbow but occasionally, white is found, which is highly unusual and rare; you are said to be VERY lucky if you are born with a 'Snowfrill'.

Parvon Teams

Parvon Teams consist of a team leader, an executive officer who is second in command, a medic, an engineer and two security specialists, one usually doubling up as communications and the other as tracking officer. This is Team Oca.

"Team Oca!" cries Team Leader Zee. "It is the twenty-fifth anniversary of our planet being made unliveable because of the Koban; we have all lost hatchmates. Our entire race is now scattered as you all know on several moons and space stations awaiting the time Randor can be revived; we were lucky, being Parvon we survived intact, on our moon when Randor was transformed into an ice ball by the two hells spawned Koban. We of Team Oca have been given a great honour. We have been chosen to go after a suspected Koban Pod." Zee lifts a clenched fist into the air, and screams, "RANDOR!"

Cheers fill the ship's recreation room where the twenty-fifth anniversary salute had been given to the dead and for the return of Randor to its former glory once the ice age is past.

Team leader Parvon Zee stands in front of his team.

He is eight feet tall and in his natural form has a lean muscled, bipedal reptilian body with a thin whip like tail, his face has a short snout and a wide mouth full of sharp serrated teeth, no one could mistake a Randorian for anything other than a carnivorous predator.

All known species of shapeshifter have the same general body type, bipedal reptiles. Only the Koban were different, being snakelike at birth and when they explosively leave a planet in order to spawn.

Zee stands proudly upright, scales flashing under the overhead lights, his tail held at attention, upright, straight behind his back. He looks over his team, they in turn see he has a pale green body, wide shoulders, narrow hips, strong arms and legs; pectoral muscles ripple as he moves his arms; black stripes run down his back; he has a red neck pouch which stretches from his chin down onto his throat (which is used during courtship rituals) and an upright frill of black feather-like fronds sticking up from crown of head trailing off to base of the neck. Painted onto his scales in bright yellow were his rank insignia. Four jagged lines on each upper arm denoting a team leader.

"I will introduce myself and the team, all of you will no doubt know each other already, but to be sure," he says with an open-handed gesture and slight bow. "I am Parvon Zee and will be your team leader."

With a wave of his arm towards the tall female to his left, he continues to speak.

"My second in command and my mate, Parvon Tona, pilot of the search ship. Vengeance."

Tona is seven feet, six inches tall, with a very lean but curvy body, wider at the hip than a male with softer facial features but still with the full complement of very sharp teeth, and as customary with all pilots she has a docked tail to allow for more comfortable seating in the pilot's chair.

She has dark green body scales, and as in all females no stripes or neck pouch. Three jagged yellow lines on each arm denote her rank of executive officer. A pure white frill (unusual for Randorians) from crown of head to nape of neck finishes off pilot Tona's looks and makes sense of her nickname since she was a hatchling, 'Snowfrill'.

Zee continues his speech with a swish of his tail; walking over he puts his hand on the shoulder of a smaller male.

"Parvon Zot, our ship's engineer and expert on the 'Stardrive 40' hyper-drive system on our ship."

Zot is seven feet tall, very slim, with pale green body scales and orange stripes down his back, a smaller red neck pouch and a crown frill of deep blue completes his appearance.

Two yellow oblongs on his upper arm denotes his rank of chief engineer. He has long articulate claw-tipped fingers.

Bringing up his other arm and placing it on the small female standing next to Zot, Zee continues.

"His mate and the ship's medic, Parvon Shna."

Shna is six feet tall and slightly chubby. She has grass, green body scales and a pale blue frill, her upper arms have a yellow-painted circle denoting the medical services of the hunter teams. Another tail flick and Zee walks around to the last pair, and with an open hand gesture towards the taller male says, "And our last pair. Parvon Zin, our weapons, tracking and security specialist."

Zin is just under eight feet of lean corded muscle; he has deep green scales with brown stripes and a scarlet throat pouch, a lighter brown crown frill decorates his skull and neck; he has two jagged yellow rank slashes on his arm.

With a last tail flick and hand motion towards the last crewmember, Zee says, "His mate and our security and navigation specialist. Parvon Ohna."

Ohna is a six foot, six-inch-tall amazon, muscles and curves in perfect proportion; she has pale green body scales, with a bright yellow crown frill decorating her head; she also has two yellow rank markers on her upper arm, denoting a senior crewman's rank, same as her mate.

Nods and murmurs of 'hellos', 'how's things', 'good to see you again' rumble around the compartment.

"We will have many cycles to get to know each other that's for sure," Zee says smiling.

Looking straight at his male security specialist, he continues.

"Zin, remember to pick up our farewell meal pack before we head out (this comprised of live Durgo lizards); it will be our last fresh taste of home for some time." Gentle purrs of laughter come from his assembled crewmates, Zin was known to forget things now and again. They would be gone for many cycles; they did not realise it would be millennia.

The Chase, 25 AIA (After Ice Age)

"Final systems check complete. All systems in the red. Launching in twenty-five beats, twenty-four, twenty-three, twenty-two…" a slow steady cadence from the pilot over the comm unit.

Five.

Four.

"I need to defecate!" Unknown wit.

"Cut the chatter!" cries Zee.

Three.

"I never paid my scale cleaner." Unknown wit number two.

"Be quiet!" growls Zee.

Two.

"I REALLY, REALLY DO NEED TO GO." Unknown wit number one.

"If I have to come back there!" snarls Zee.

"PARRRP!" (Farting noise over the speaker) Groans of 'phew' and 'arrrg', 'what's that smell', followed by giggles.

One! LAUNCH. "It's going to be a long mission," said Zee sighing.

Cycle One (Day One), Ship Time

"Tell me it's not true, by the two hells, Shna, tell me." Ohna's tail is swishing side to side, sure sign of stress.

"It's true! He has scalemites," replies the medic.

"AAARRRRG!" It was only through using all her will power that Ohna did not start scratching herself right away.

"Scalemites! Where in the two hells did, he pick them up, has the scale-dipped cretin not heard of scale cleaners? AAAAAAARRRRGGG!" She starts scratching.

"So, Shna has the pair of them isolated, everyone else is to be checked, the ship is to be cleansed by a light bombardment of radiation and chemical cleaners. Hells, what a way to start the mission!" groans Zee with an angry flick of his tail.

"It could be worse," said the tailless pilot absently scratching her arm.

"The whole crew? THE-WHOLE-CREW? By the two hells! I will peel the scales off the scale-dipped idiot one at a time." Zee's tail is going back and forth too fast to see.

"Yes, team leader, all of us, we are all going to be miserable for the next few cycles," said an unhappy medic scratching her frill.

It turned out that Zin had picked up the nasty little parasites the day before launch from the delivery female that had dropped off their going away meal pack; she had insisted on a farewell hug.

Ohna was not happy about the delivery method, and only viewing security footage stopped Ohna from removing a particular male body part from the bug carrier.

No one was going to let Zin forget this incident in a hurry, that was for sure.

Cycle Four, Ship Time

The ship smelled of chemical cleaner, and every crew members' scales gleamed (The only good thing to come out of it).

The Randorians did not wear clothes, so nothing else needed cleaning, harnesses were worn to carry equipment, spacesuits were not required, just breathing gear, and so the ship was cleansed rather faster than its crew…Zin was in the gobal house.

"You scale-dipped idiot, you get your gobal de-loused once a month to stop this kind of thing, maybe we should start doing that with you; I never stopped scratching for three cycles. THREE! THREE CYCLES!" Ohna's tail was a blur.

"HOW CAN THIS BE MY FAULT? I WAS THE ONE ORDERED TO GO PICK UP THE MEAL PACK…ORDERED, MIND YOU, ORDERED…NOT—MY—FAULT!" cries Zin, storming away, tail held up rigid against his back.

"CONTACT," the ship's speaker alerts the crew. The chase is on.

"Where, Snowfrill?" asks Zee, tail twitching nervously.

"Heading into the third arm of our spiral galaxy, TXP73. We need to get closer to see which planet." Tail stub bouncing side to side with excitement.

"Head in, best speed," orders Zee.

Far in front of them, the Koban pod is heading towards a planet teaming with life and just as important. Water, lots of water.

The pod is forty feet long and lozenge shaped, blue black in colour and houses a single creature which ejects itself into space by using a geothermal explosion from an active volcano. (This can have a disastrous effect on a planet as witnessed by the ice age Randor was put into.) It then travels at ejection velocity in suspended animation until it finds another planetary food source. It then lands and stocks up, eating massive amounts of food over many months until she is ready to lay eggs. Hundreds, sometimes even thousands, of eggs. They hatch in batches at different times depending on outside stimuli. Each hatching brood then has an equal chance with the available food sources at hand. The mother then leaves for another planet to start the cycle all over again.

The third planet from this particular sun was about to get an unwanted guest. The planet had several large land masses, the rest was water. Most unusual. Planets up till now have all been quite arid, hence the reptilian nature of the dominant species so far found in the galaxy. The pod hit a large land mass near its southern tip, the impact of the almost indestructible pod's outer casing driving it deep underground.

The Koban pod splits open and tentacle-like appendages come out from all sides; it starts to burrow and enlarge the space; it then produces secretions like spider silk, strengthening the walls to make a nest-like chamber. The Koban entity has used up most of its energy, and mass. It rests before burrowing to the surface of its new home.

The Koban like all shapeshifters can only shift into something of the same mass and it needs to physically touch whatever it shifts into, subsuming its host and becoming an exact replica, memories and skills intact, the shift melds the two forms together leaving only the new host, the previous body is gone, totally absorbed.

The Koban female surfaces cautiously into a vast undulating grassland teaming with life.

Most are herbivores, but the herbivores are prey to carnivores, just what the large female requires.

The Koban needs protein, lots of protein.

It selects a predator close to its mass. A near perfect match.

The Koban is just under sixty-five feet long, with a tapered snakelike body, slithering through the grass, it quickly gets to within ten feet of the large carnivore, which is totally absorbed in eating a fresh kill. The Spinosaurus that the Koban female has selected is huge, near on twenty tons and fifty feet high; its head alone is six feet long.

A killing machine.

Now let's make it an intelligent killing machine.

The Spinosaurus never knew what hit it. The Koban strikes cobra quick. Its four hooked teeth latching onto the Spinosaurus inserting hundreds of fine tendrils under its scales, and within thirty beats, the shift has taken effect.

This is when all shapeshifters are vulnerable, as they have no control over the new body until the shift is complete, but all goes well.

Over the next sixty cycles of the planet, the Spinosaurus/Koban decimates the herds of grass eaters, and any predators who are stupid enough to challenge it. With all this protein, its bulk increases; it is now time for her to lay eggs.

Koban Hatchlings

The Koban mother lays eggs in clutches of twenty to forty at a time, widely spaced out. The Koban/Spinosaurus travels constantly driven by instinct, laying eggs and eating. Not needing to sleep, the big animal covers a vast distance in a short time; just over seven thousand eggs are laid; by the time the Koban is nearly finished, the first batch of thirty eggs she laid earlier, hatch. Instinct drives the snakelike young to find a host, the inquisitive small Velociraptors found in abundance in the area become a favoured first host.

The Koban's eggs are usually the size of footballs, though some smaller ones sometimes get laid; when this happens, the small shapeshifter rarely survives its first weeks, falling prey to stronger predators. The eggs are soft when first laid but quickly harden to a material similar to the mother's escape pod shell, virtually unbreakable as the local raptors and small egg-eating predators find out by spending many beats trying to break into the eggs.

On hatching, the tiny predators search for hosts. Once they all achieve this, they hunt as a pack taking down larger and larger prey animals. Constantly searching for better hosts as their body size slowly increases. Newly hatched Koban are one to three feet long. Most new hatchlings subsume small Velociraptors and with their higher functioning brains turned these little predators into something far more deadly. They obliterate the local dinosaur herds.

The Koban's natural form is snakelike. It has a long, tapered body but its head is somewhat bulbous; it has a small circular mouth with four hook like teeth, which have only one function, to latch on and grip something. Of all the shapeshifters, the Koban are unique, they are true parasites, they cannot survive in their original form, they must find a host to survive and grow.

Around the mouth are hundreds of very fine tendrils; it is these that burrow under scales and transmit the enzyme which first paralyses the host then transfers the Koban into the host organism's body. The transformation or shift can take from ten to forty beats or seconds. As this is happening, the Koban or any other shapeshifter for that matter is totally helpless.

The Koban cannot keep its original form and prefers two-legged upright creatures if it can get them. It only reverts to its original form to leave the planet as a fully mature female, ready to give birth to the next generation of Koban, only females can transform, the males are only there to supply the females with sperm which is stored until it is fertilised by the same chemical transformation returning the mother to its snakelike form.

Cycle Sixty-Two, Ship Time (Approaching the Third Planet from the System Primary)

"THIS IS IT! There is still a trace of trylixan given off from the Gravitox ejection event, the only planet with life is just ahead; we will be orbiting within a cycle, tell the scale mite to get ready." Snowfrill's tail stump was bouncing with glee.

"It's been sixty cycles, give it a rest already, how many times do I have to say sorry?" Laughs come from the speaker. Zin walks away, his tail dragging behind on the floor.

"INSERTION! We are in geo-sync orbit above the strongest signal strength," crackles over the ship's comes from Tona.

"Away, team! Assemble in the armoury!" cries Zee over the command comm.

Zin and Ohna fully geared up with harnesses filled with food, water and an assortment of weapons ease themselves into the dropships pilot and co-pilot seats, making sure their tails fit through the slot in the padded chair.

"Gear check, Ohna! Phase rifles."

"Check."

"Side arms."

"Check."

"Food bars, if you can call them that?"

"Check." (Giggles)

"Water! Twenty gulps, recycled water that is!"

"Check." (Open laughter)

"First aid kit, to handle the food poisoning and god knows what from the recycled. I don't even want to call it, water."

"Check." (Gurgles of mirth)

"Comms gear, to get us help when we are stuck defecating our tails off, see above list of pathogens."

"Check." (Open guffaws)

"YOU TWO HATCHLINGS FINISHED?" cries Zee (Murmurs just off range of the mic, Zee can be heard saying, "Hatchlings, I have a crew of scale-blighted hatchlings.")

"Eh-hem! Right, ookay, let's go then, ehhh! What button do I press again, Ohna?" Professional sounding, really professional sounding. (Giggles can be heard in the background.)

The dropship spirals down to land in an open area surrounded by low hills, no sign of life on the bio tracker, but there are bones everywhere.

"Team One to Team Lead, no signs of life, but it's a killing field down here; there are bones everywhere," reports Zin.

"Look for the nest, it will be a cave or hole in the side of a hill, use heat tracking, it will put out a lot of heat, be careful, and if you bring us up anymore, little friends. The airlock will stay shut." Giggles could be heard just before the comms shut down.

"How long am I going to get this SHIT? One mistake, Ohna, one mistake."

Ohna laughs softly. "Let's find this abomination and go home."

They both separate by a few lengths and scan the terrain; it is not long before a heat bloom is picked up on sensors. It leads them both to a cave opening. The smell of rotting flesh is strong enough to make them gag.

"We have found an entrance, coordinates as follows, 100.76 by 80.04. Do we strike from orbit, or do we go in and plant a destructor bomb? Zin out."

"No risks, Zin, come back up, we will take it out with a kinetic, Zee out."

Back on board, Zin and Ohna watch as the kinetic weapon is brought to bear on the cave. The magnetic rail gun will send a chunk of metal at super high velocity destroying all in its path.

"Fire control locked, safety disengaged, firing on your command, Team Lead," says Tona.

Zee nods over to Tona. "Fire!"

On the screen, a bright bloom of light shows the end of whatever was in that area, a sixty-foot deep crater is all that's left.

"Go back down, search for signs of life, get some biomass for me to study if possible," says Shna.

The search of the area showed no sign of anything recoverable, forty units away a mother senses a loss, triggering the female's natural defence towards its young.

Laying another clutch of eggs, she goes to find out what happened to her hatchling.

"Keep monitoring the area, see what shows up. Tona! Start a grid search, look for concentrations of live animals." Zee turns and walks to his cabin, not to sleep, the species don't do anything as stupid as that, he has reports to compile.

"CONTACT! Large mass of animals, co-ordinates being sent to the dropship, Tona out."

"Landing party to the dropship, co-ordinates have been downloaded to your screen." Zee turns from the comms unit and sprints to the lander bay, all bar the pilot Tona would be going down this time.

The dropship lands on a small hill overlooking a valley full of slowly moving dinosaurs of varying sizes, quietly eating away at the grass and bushes.

Shna walks down the ramp from the dropship, stretches her arms straight up and takes in a deep breath through her nose. "Smell that air! So much better than recycled."

"Smells like shit! There are multitudes of shitting beasts out there," replies Zot, not a nature lover.

Taking in another long slow breath, Shna smiles and replies, "Still smells good."

"URGH, I just stepped in some of your nice-smelling air." Zot shakes his foot wildly, shit flies everywhere.

"Better get that off your toes before we go back in the dropship," the medic says with a grin.

"YECH!" Zot manically scrubs his feet with grass.

"Stop the chatter!" cries Zee. "Concentrate on the job."

"Still smells nice." Shna giggles.

"SHNA!" growls Zee.

"Okay," a small voice returns with giggles in the background.

"I HAVE A CREW FULL OF HATCHLINGS." Zee walks on, shaking his head.

"CONTACT FRONT!" No nonsense, professional sounding. Zin brings up his phase rifle in one smooth move, looks through the holographic sight and sees.

A huge animal bursts through the grazers. Its large head full of teeth sitting atop a strong body with small arms and muscular legs. It screams a challenge at the team as they stand next to the dropship, and charges forward, head lowered, mouth gaping wide, saliva spraying as it runs.

Zin calmly pulls the trigger, a bolt of bright blue energy goes through the creature's head, dropping it instantly dead. They all go forward to view the animal.

"Stop!" cries Ohna. "Don't you touch that?"

Zin backs off, a puzzled look on his face.

"Look, you Durgo-brained scale scrubber, it's got scalemites!"

"By the two hells, not again," moans Zin. The rest burst out laughing.

Across the other side of the hill, two intelligent eyes watch from the subsumed Spinosaurus. The Koban mother comes up with a plan; she has lain just over seven thousand eggs, scattered over every part of the large land mass and has eaten enough food to trans configure into the ejection pod and leave this planet for its young to plunder.

She must destroy the hunters to give her hatchlings a chance of survival though.

It's how to get the ship she knows is in orbit to land, that will be tricky. But she has a plan.

Using ultra-low frequency soundwaves unique to the Koban she calls to one of her young. Within moments, a small eight-foot dinosaur is at its mother's side.

"Consume the large one with the black stripes. Shift into its form. I can sense it is the leader, then come back to me," growls the Koban mother.

"Team Lead! Tona. I am in geosynchronous orbit overhead; there is a large heat bloom showing on my scanners to your south, just inside the treeline; I do not know what it is?"

"Thanks, Snowfrill, we will check it out." Zee turns towards his team. "Spread out, be careful."

They move across the undulating grass. Just as Zee enters a slight dip and goes out of sight of the others, he is tackled from behind, fine hair like tendrils enter his scales just like the mites did. Thirty beats later, Zee is not quite himself anymore; looking around, he heads for his mother. She tells him the plan.

"Team Lead to crew, gather at the dropship, something has happened."

The Koban mother goes to her underground chamber, her body mass, now sufficient after taking in so much food, is ready to leave the planet. She starts to revert back to her snakelike natural form. Her young, once hatched will scatter and shift into the first suitable host they can find. Growth is slow, it will take thousands of cycles for them to reach full maturity.

Unhatched eggs will stay dormant, hatching in small clutches of ten to forty hatchlings over the next thousand or so cycles.

She starts to transform into the space travel pod. Having transitioned back into her natural serpentine shape, she coils into a tight ball. The super hard exterior starts to form around her just like a caterpillar forming its cocoon.

"I was going to use the dropship for overhead surveillance. Something is wrong, it won't start, check it out, Zot." The bogus Zee stands still, looking at his crew.

"Will do, Team Lead, let me and Zin check it out." Zot ducks inside fiddling with various components and plugging in a diagnostics reader. Zin holds a light illuminating the underside of the panel for Zot to see better.

"Found it! We have a faulty igniter diode, easy fix; it has pins misaligned, we just need the spare from the ship." (Protocol states the igniter module must be replaced rather than repaired for safety reasons.)

"Team Lead to Tona, bring the ship down to these coordinates."

The Koban/Zee hears a low-level buzz in his ear.

"Excellent, find a safe place to hide my hatchling, you will need to be far away from me when I depart, make an excuse to leave the rest, I will signal you before escaping this planet."

"Okay, team, while we are here, we will try to find where this Koban has set up. We will split into groups, be back when Tona lands. Zin, you and Ohna go west. Zot, you come with me. Shna, stay here as medical back up. Everyone, call in regular. Let's go." Bogus Zee walks away with Zot trailing behind, giving a farewell wave and smile to Shna.

"Zin, come over here please, I want to try out the new AI interface while we have the chance. We should be able to field test it over various distances once I have inserted it into your head."

"Okay, Shna, I'll be over in a beat." Zin trots over to the medic.

"One question! Will it hurt, Shna?"

"No, it won't hurt, Zin."

"AAARRRRGGGGH! TWO HELLS, THAT HURT!"

"Cryhatchling, okay, let me check the interface."

"POP! AWWGG! That hurt worse."

"You have a low pain threshold even for a male, did you hear anything, Zin?"

"Yes, a popping noise."

"That's it! Zin, it should be good. The popping noise was the computer interface going through your skull bone."

"Eww! Too much information, Shna."

"Okay, let's test it out, Zin, then you are free to go, just listen! It should be like someone talking in your ear, you can answer sub-vocally or speak out loud, it's up to you."

"HELLO, ZIN, I AM, I AM? IIIEEE? I DON'T HAVE A NAME?"

"It's asking for a name what do I call it?"

"Anything you want really," Shna says with a shrug. "With this unit, you can give it a full personality if you like, keep it simple for now, just call it 'HELP'."

"Okay? Hi, your name for now is 'HELP'."

"THAT'S NICE, HI, ZIN. MY NAME IS HELP."

So, all the teams went to their designated sectors to scout the area for the Koban. Zin and Ohna along with a constantly questioning 'Help' headed for theirs.

"MY DATA BANKS HAVE NO REFERENCE TO ANY OF THESE CREATURES OR PLANT LIFE, WHAT'S THAT?"

"Don't know," murmurs Zin.

"WHAT'S THIS?" exited exclamation from Help.

"Don't know." Zin sighs.

"OOOHH WHAT'S THAT?" asks an awe-sounding Help.

"Still don't know," groans Zin.

This went on constantly, by a half cycle it was driving him nuts.

"This isn't working!" cries a frustrated Zin.

"Team Lead, to all personnel! Head back to the dropship."

As everyone gathered back at the dropship, the roar of re-entry from the 'Vengeance' could be heard.

Looking up, the crew watch the large ship coming down to rest well clear of the dropship; with a muffled thump, the big ship lands.

Pings and ticks of cooling metal could be heard as the ship settled.

"Wait here while I go talk to Tona," came over the comms channel from the bogus Zee.

"ATTENTION, ZIN! THAT IS NOT TEAM LEADER ZEE."

"WHAT?" snaps Zin.

"THE VOICE MODULATION IS WRONG; SOMEONE IS FAKING HIS VOICE."

"How can that be possible?" mumbles a confused Zin.

"THE ONLY POSSIBILITY IS HE HAS BEEN SUBSUMED BY A SHAPESHIFTER."

Back at the grounded ship.

"Hi, Zee, what do you need me down for, did you miss me that much?" Tona says with a loving smile looking over her shoulder at the approaching bogus Zee. Snowfrill is suddenly no longer lucky.

Zee shoots her in the face twice without breaking stride.

Turning around, he heads back to the rest of the team, locking the airlock with his security override as he goes.

"THAT WAS A PHASE PISTOL SHOT."

"I never heard anything?" Zin cries looking frantically around.

"I DID, ZEE IS RETURNING."

"What now?" questions Zin.

"ZEE HAS SHOT SHNA," says a matter-of-fact sounding Help.

Jumping down from the dropship, Zin screams out for Ohna and Zot.

Only Ohna comes over.

"We are in trouble, Ohna! The Koban have gotten to Zee. I think Tona and Shna are dead."

They run towards the large ship only to find it securely locked. On the way back to the dropship, they find Shna. Zin grabs her harness.

She has been shot twice in the head! And is obviously dead. Near the back of the dropship lying face down, they find Zot, shot the same way.

Zin grabs Zot's repair harness and tools, then bolts up the dropship gangplank into the ship.

Calling out for Ohna, he sees her turn at some unheard noise, then. BANG!

A burst of blood shoots from her head and she falls into the ship.

Zin hits the door close switch and runs for Ohna, dragging her further into the ship as the ramp closed, leaving a smear of blood on the deck plates.

Outside, the shapeshifted Zee gets the message from his mother.

"Flee, my hatchling, you have a cycle before I leave."

"OHNA!" screams Zin, rocking back and forth with Ohna in his arms. "I NEED HELP, SOMEBODY HELP!"

"WHAT DO YOU REQUIRE, ZIN?"

"Help! Do something," pleads Zin, tears streaking his face.

"SHE IS TERMINAL, THERE IS NOTHING THAT CAN BE DONE FOR HER BODY," reports Help.

"What can we do?" sobs Zin.

"TRANSFER HER ESSENCE USING THE PERSONALITY UNIT IN SHNA'S EQUIPMENT."

"Tell me what to do." Zin is devastated.

Zin got all of Shna's gear and laid it all out to Help's specifications.

Zin hooks up the dying Ohna's brain to the transfer module.

"EVERYTHING IS SET. I DO NOT KNOW HOW MUCH PAIN THIS WILL CAUSE, BUT YOU WILL FEEL SOMETHING THAT'S FOR SURE. THIS IS SO MUCH MORE THAN WHEN MY BASIC FORM WAS INSERTED. THIS SETUP EVEN HAS A HOLOGRAPHIC AVATAR. ARE YOU READY, ZIN? IT HAS BEEN GOOD KNOWING YOU, GOODBYE, ZIN." The sad sounding pleasant voice of Help.

Pop!

Darkness.

Then a pinpoint of light.

Zin awakens to the unexpected voice of his dead mate.

"I HAVE A HEADACHE! WHAT YOU HAVE DONE TO ME, YOU SCALE-SCRUBBING BANDGUB?"

"Ohna, I can hear you! Are you okay?"

"TWO HELLS! OF COURSE, I AM NOT OKAY! LOOK AT ME! I AM DEAD! YOU LIMP-TAILED IDIOT."

"This is going to take some getting used to," says a befuddled Zin.

"I AM DETECTING A MASSIVE GRAVITOX BUILD UP NEARBY. WE NEED TO MOVE...NOW!"

Zin jumps into the pilot's seat, feels around under the console and pops out the igniter module, knowing from helping Zot that it has only misaligned pins and has been disconnected, a quick reinsertion of pins and the unit is re-installed, the engines start immediately.

He takes off and flies over a nearby mountain range, landing in a dry riverbed.

The Koban mother has dug down into a vent leading to a vast underground super volcano. The blast is huge! Hurtling the pod into space. Leaving a one-hundred-and-ten-mile diameter crater in what would be known as the Yucatan Peninsula. Destroying the Vengeance and killing everything within hundreds of miles including the bogus Zee who had not moved as quickly as he should have, and causing what scientist believe in the future to be the extinction of the dinosaurs?

It was not!

The Koban young in their thousands did that.

Safe within the dropship, Parvon Zin and his acid-tongued AI wait out the aftermath.

Aftermath. Cycle Sixty-Nine, Ship Time

Zin and Ohna wait out the after effects of the huge explosion that sent the Koban mother into space. Protected by the bulk of the mountain range, they landed behind; they ride out the explosion with no damage at all. Zin has to go outside several times to clear ash from the dropship, but other than that, they were okay.

It has been totally dark for three cycles, the ash has stopped falling, but the atmosphere is laden with it, blocking out the sun. Fearing being trapped or the shuttle being damaged, Zin takes off and heads for orbit.

Low TXP73 S-3 Orbit

Zin puts the dropship into geosynchronous orbit over the Koban escape crater. It is huge! He can see it from orbit! He can also make out the ash plume drifting with the prevailing East wind over the open water. Time to take stock, Zin checks out what he has by way of supplies and equipment.

"Okay, Ohna! What do we have to survive with on this primitive dirtball of a planet? Good enough name that! We will call it 'Dirtball'."

Ohna's avatar stands in mockery of the actual Ohna, a lump forms in Zin's throat. "I miss you so much."

"WHAT DO YOU MEAN, SCALEMITE? I AM STILL HERE! IT'S STILL ME! JUST NOT IN BODY, I FEEL JUST THE SAME. IT'S WEIRD? I JUST CAN'T TOUCH ANYTHING, I CAN SEE, HEAR, FEEL TO A DEGREE THROUGH THE SENSORS IN YOUR HEAD AND IN ANY SENSOR HARDWARE WE HAVE, SO DON'T DESPAIR, YOU SAVED ME. I WILL ALWAYS BE HERE WITH YOU, SO GET YOUR CLAW OUT OF YOUR CLOACA AND LET'S WORK THIS OUT, WE HAVE THOUSANDS OF KOBAN TO KILL TO AVENGE OUR CREWMATES."

"Thanks, Ohna, you may need to keep telling me that from time to time, so what have we got?"

"THE COMPUTER SAYS WE HAVE ALMOST A FULL TANK OF FUEL, RATION AND WATER PACKS FOR THIRTY CYCLES, BUT THAT WAS FOR A SIX-PARVON CREW, SO WE HAVE ONE HUNDRED AND EIGHTY CYCLES OF SUPPLIES. REMEMBER, I DON'T EAT SO IT'S ALL YOURS. WEAPONS, TWO PHASE RIFLES, TWO SIDE ARMS, TWO TRAVEL HARNESSES WITH KNIFE, WATER BOTTLE, FIRST AID AND SENSOR KIT. LIGHT UNIT, SOLAR CHARGER AND THREE HUNDRED UNITS OF ULTRA-TWIST CLIMBING LINE, SEE WHAT YOU CAN FIND INSIDE THE CABIN."

Zin does a thorough check of the cabin and comes up with Zot's tool harness, Shna's medical harness and emergency pack plus the trans-essence unit for the AI hook-up. Looking through personal crew lockers, he finds additional multi-use battery packs, food bars (in Shna's locker) lots of food bars. *No wonder you were chunky*, Zin thinks to himself with a smile. In the command locker, he finds 'Gold dust!', two hyper-comm units in their sturdy tamperproof metal containers.

"OH YES! We can call for pick up, Ohna! We will be out of here before you know it."

He breathes into the security grid and the case opens, a quick check and Zin hits the transmit button.

"Parvon Zin, calling command. Emergency extraction required from TXP73-S3 sole survivor of team Oca please respond." …Static!

"Repeat! Team Oca. Emergency extraction from TXP73-S3 COME IN!" …STATIC!

"I will keep trying, Ohna, we are a fair distance from anyone, after all, so it might take a while." (If only he knew.)

Further search of the ship uncovers little else of use, some music and video files, two bottles of booze smuggled on by who knows? Might have been Zot, he liked a drink, rap around eye light filters, which would come in handy. Zin did not like strong sunlight and this planet's sun was much brighter than Randor's had been.

"Well, Ohna, that's what we have, there is no point in landing on the continent where thousands of hungry, vicious Koban are; we would not last a cycle, we will land on the other side of the planet and let the wildlife here whittle down their numbers a bit."

So, with that, Zin pilots the dropship for a landing in what will be Turkey, Southern Europe.

Cruising at two hundred feet, Zin selects a cliff top mesa and brings the craft into land, his flyby shows plenty of animal life and abundant water, this would do for the short time it would take before rescue. (YEAH, RIGHT!)

The Anunnaki and the Rise of the 'Highbrows'

"ZIN, I AM PICKING UP A PROBE IN ORBIT, IT DOES NOT RESPOND TO STANDARD HAILS? WHO CAN IT BE?"

"No idea, Ohna, where is it?"

"SOUTH OF US IN GEOSYNCHRONOUS ORBIT ABOVE THIS CONTINENT; IT IS STARTING TO LAND."

"Let's go check it out, we may get off this rock earlier than we thought," muses Zin.

They lift off and head south towards what will be Iraq. Zin lands the shuttle on top of a mountain ridge overlooking the large dropship-sized probe; it has small tracked vehicles coming out of both side doors. The little vehicles scream off in different directions, it is obvious from their vantage point that the vehicles are gathering samples, dirt, rock, flora and bipedal primates, several different types. Zin watches for five cycles, he notes the type of craft to be from the Planet Niberu. Anunnaki, shape shifters who lust after gold and other precious metals and have no qualms about how they get it.

They are despised throughout the Spiral Galaxy systems for being totally ruthless, destroying planets by their total disregard for anything bar their profit, strip mining the planets bare.

"We are in trouble if the Anunnaki come here, Ohna. The scale-blighted Koban are bad enough, these scale ticks will kill us on sight. We need to be cautious and watch what they do.”

Next day, the probe blasted off and headed to who knows where? It was out of range within a cycle.

A month later and Ohna picks up a huge signal as a craft comes into orbit.

It can easily be seen with the naked eye; through the dropship’s scanner it is seen to be a huge, mining ship full of everything the Anunnaki needs to strip an area bare.

They return to the spot they had been before and Zin witness the Anunnaki start to work on the area they have chosen to be their headquarters and mine site.

Buildings are fabricated, landing areas are cleared and levelled, hundreds of tracked vehicles head out to start taking further samples in areas they previously scouted with the first probe collecting the local primates, raw ore and minerals.

Zin puts this down to gathering a food stock, but that soon becomes something else when he notices the teams of medical and scientific personnel that are gathering at a very large structure that has been built beside two rivers that flow through the area.

Animal pens are constructed, and the various primates are herded into each and separated by species; within a couple of cycles of testing an obvious favourite seems to have been chosen, a more upright standing less hairy primate, further proof that this type of primate is reserved for something else is noticed as the other primates start to be devoured in typical shapeshifter fashion. ‘Chase and kill’ events. (Muscle that has been worked has more blood in it, it makes it juicier.)

These take place every cycle as groups are removed from pens and chased down and devoured.

The other group are fed into the large building fifty at a time, the ones that come out the other end are vastly different from when they went in. Genetically altered by the advanced medical and scientifically advanced Anunnaki into a useable slave species.

They are now fully upright, less hairy and are being trained, rather brutally using shock sticks, to do simple tasks like digging, collecting soil spill and filling hoppers. It does not take long for these creatures to learn and avoid pain. They are also well fed when they perform as instructed, this technique works very quickly and in no time at all they have a sizeable workforce to dig in the mines.

Zin and Ohna are forced to leave the area as the landing site expands at an alarming rate, and security branches out nearer their hide; they head north and assess their situation.

The Anunnaki with their trained workforce of slaves, known as 'Adamu', now start to really work the area for precious minerals, gold, silver and gems.

To keep the Adamu under control, they introduce 'Worship' of themselves as 'GODS'. This is done throughout their training, so it is now second nature to the simple Adamu, and they do this without thinking, it is just the way of things, they think of nothing else.

'ANU' is to be their 'Sky God' and is worshipped daily with every meal that is eaten reinforcing the effect; this works so well that the Anunnaki's stay on Earth lasts thousands of years and is without any problems from the Adamu slave population.

Anunnaki overseers are in place for thousands of years at a time, the immortal shapeshifters being able to do this easily, so generations of slave workers know nothing else, for them it is normal.

The first 'God/Ruler' was called 'Alulim', his contract as planetary overseer lasted twenty-eight thousand eight hundred years. During this time under Anunnaki control and guidance, vast cities are made from stone using mechanical lifting and cutting tools.

The next overseer was called 'Alaljar', his contract ran for thirty-six thousand years. During his time, the final genetic additions to the Adamu slave workers was completed and this new worker species was intelligent enough to follow higher level instruction in order to more successfully mine the area.

There are four hundred and eighty-seven Anunnaki working at the site as trainers, overseers and security troops. The Koban, this clutch had arrived in the area by boat some time ago, chance upon the operation and do their thing; working in small packs they overpower the Anunnaki individually, and within several cycles, the Koban have taken over the Anunnaki mine site. The Adamu slave population have no idea anything is wrong and follow commands as usual. The Anunnaki mine is in a place known as Sumer.

The Sumerian city of Ur is turned into the Koban's capital, the Koban can't believe what they have gotten themselves and live it large throwing massive parties and festivals; production levels start to drop, this flags up as a problem and is automatically reported back to Nibiru.

The investigating officer from Nibiru runs scans of the area and quickly picks up traces of Koban infection, this becomes evident when his craft comes under fire from the mine site's security guns; he quickly returns to orbit to report.

A full scan from orbit shows that all of the original Anunnaki present on site have been subsumed, the only option is to cleanse the infected area, just to be sure.

Ur is laid waste by an orbital bombardment of seven atomic warheads, destroying the city and the Koban presence within.

Ohna picks up the nuclear explosions on the scanners; they have no idea what has happened; they are forced to stay away from the Anunnaki site now because of the upgraded security surrounding it, and so the pair of them stay hidden and let history play itself out.

The Anunnaki stay on the planet for another one hundred thousand years, until they strip out all of the gold, precious metals and gems they could get. They then simply pack up and leave.

Interbreeding between the Adamu slaves has produced slightly smarter people, but most are just bright animals no smarter than a well-trained dog. With the departure of their gods and a promise that they will return, the Adamu scatter and form tribes and separate peoples up and down the Middle-East; they eventually come across the Neanderthal, and to them, they are known as 'Highbrows'.

Rise of the Koban

Hundreds of eggs had hatched and subsumed small predators, usually Velociraptors or something similar sized.

It was so easy! The victims just lay there? Not moving at all!

It soon becomes known among the Koban using their unique ultra-low frequency signalling that the creatures of this planet for some weird reason go dormant for long periods of time, during darkness and even in full daylight.

The Koban hatchlings have found an ultra-safe food source on this planet, one that doesn't fight back injuring or killing their attackers.

Hundreds become thousands; thousands become several. All in all, there are seven thousand three hundred and seventy-eight Koban on the planet.

The Koban wipe out entire species. First to go were the large Sauropods, slow moving, easy kills, with a huge amount of meat on the carcass.

If the Koban ran into trouble with predators or more dangerous herd animals, it was a simple matter of retreating and waiting till they went dormant. Within a few sun cycles, all the large predators and herbivores on this part of the continent are gone.

The Koban now hunt in super packs of sixty to one hundred, killing entire herds in one night. Alpha females run the packs.

1000 Sun Cycles Pass

The Koban still number in the several thousands; very few have fallen to predators or accidents, but now, Kobans are being killed! Heads have been found impaled on pieces of tree branches as warnings.

Alpha females gather and discuss this new phenomenon, they have no names for each other, all are known by the pheromone scent released by each Koban; the scent is totally unique to the individual. That changes with the first meeting of the 'Draconians'.

Draconians

With the extinction of all but a few large predators, smaller more intelligent creatures emerge. The Draconians are a bipedal small-snouted upright-standing dinosaur, but it has a larger brain, two opposable thumbs and it used tools; it could think! This made it a very successful lifeform indeed.

Draconians gathered in family or clan groups, they build defensive structures of sharpened stakes, or fortify caves with piled up stones to protect themselves; they discover fire and live comfortably through the cold winters. They flourish.

They also have a rudimentary language and call each other by name.

One such Clan known as 'The Red Cave Clan' lived atop a small rise in a series of interlinked caves formed from red sandstone giving the caves their distinctive look and name. The caves overlooked a sheltered cove with a gentle sloping beach; the 'Red Caves' hunted fish in its shallow warm waters.

They were celebrating the destruction of a nasty pack of six Velociraptors that had been terrorising their land. Pit traps had been dug previously as defence against large predators; these were eight feet deep, and the tops covered in thin branches and covered in leaves; the pits protected the easy route up to the caves. Six Koban/Velociraptors were caught in the traps and stoned to death by the clan's guards. The heads had been left as warnings to any other predator coming onto Red Cave territory, a 'Beware, do not mess with us' sign if you like.

The 'Red Caves' posted lookouts when the clan slept, this saved the clan from the initial attack of the Koban Velociraptors when they noisily fell into the pits but guaranteed its destruction when the Koban's only survivor from the scouting party reported back to the alpha females, the Koban realise they have stumbled upon their first sentient creatures since hatching.

Exactly what is sought in order to advance.

The Draconians end up being the Koban's favoured body form and is used throughout their time on this planet, right up until humans gain dominance.

Flinexa is a small female Draconian barely past hatchling size, on tip claws she is three feet high, just the right size for a Koban Raptor to take.

Flinexa is known for wandering away and sleeping under the stars; being very intelligent, the young female looks up and wonders what all the pinpoints of light are. She is taken mid-ponder by a small female Koban/Raptor, thirty beats later and the female Koban/Draconian says to herself, "My name it seems is Flinexa? I like the sound of that."

There are seventy-four individual Draconians in the clan. The two guards are taken first, all the rest are subsumed as they sleep.

The Koban with their superior brains and now with a body they can manipulate and create things with, have no limits as to what they can do.

They quickly realise that all of their brood mates need to be in this body form. Using their unique low frequency soundwave growl, signals are sent out.

All of the Draconian type of upright walking sentient dinosaurs are actively sought out. Within a few cycles, every Koban has taken over a Draconian and now have the superior body form.

There are still thousands of Koban alive, all of which are now scattered in every Draconian clan group throughout the bottom end of the large continental mass that will eventually be South America.

Thousands of years pass. The Koban are now the ruling elite of a vast Draconian nation. Covering the coastal regions in the south right up to the heavily forested centre which is way too dangerous to try and conquer due to the thickness of the jungle and the animals adapted to survive in it.

The Koban/Draconians are well loved as benevolent, fair, gentle rulers, as long as you are Draconian that is.

With the Koban's intelligent ruling of the Draconians, their dominance in the area is ensured.

Food stocks are maintained as animal husbandry is introduced; water is piped in to give every household fresh running water; fire to heat the water is used to give each dwelling under tile heating, hot baths and saunas to clean scales; it is a very advanced culture that is springing up; domesticated dinosaurs are used for transport and heavy lifting; no one goes hungry and the Koban find themselves in as perfect a position as a parasitic lifeform can get.

Plenty of food and a safe environment.

The Draconians love their leaders and celebrate that love with festivals using fireworks that the Koban/Draconians developed as a novelty to impress the locals. Salt peter, sulphur and charcoal are mixed up to produce flashes of light and puffs of smoke, the Draconians loved it.

All is going great, until the smelly, smooth-skinned 'THINGS' turned up.

Fall of Draconia

It started small as most things usually do. In this case, it was an eight strong Draconian fishing party on the coast catching fish with thrown nets. One said, "WHAT'S THAT HORRIBLE SMELL?"

Then all hell broke loose.

Neanderthal Raiding Force, 'Keeka'

Keeka was the leader of this seaborne Neanderthal raiding/exploration force that discovered the Draconian fishing party.

Standing at nearly eight feet, Keeka was a heavily muscled, perfect specimen of his tribe 'The Errin'.

He has a low-browed forehead with dark brown skin, heavy black hair covering most of it, a mono-eyebrow shading light brown intelligent eyes, cured animal skins cover his loins, and in his hand is an axe made from an animal's lower jaw. He has a large skull with brain to match, which the Neanderthals use to make them the dominant lifeform in their area. Houses, boatbuilding, tool making, a structured society, making them a very successful culture indeed.

Keeka is a very intelligent being and has risen to the rank of raider leader because of it.

Sixty Neanderthal raiders had landed on the coast after having sailed across the ocean searching for new much-needed lands.

The Neanderthals hated and feared dinosaurs, because of what was happening back home in Erra (present day South Africa). It was a constant struggle to survive the onslaught of large predators that thrived on the flat plains of their homeland, amongst the teaming herds of grazing plant-eating dinosaurs, forcing the Errin to hug the coastal strip in wooden walled villages, reliant on the sea for survival. To leave the protection of the walled villages was to die, consumed by the dinosaurs. (Many had tried and a wall of names was erected to commemorate their sacrifice.) So, when they came across the fishing party of eight Draconians, they slaughtered them without remorse.

The Errin numbered in the hundreds of thousands and were looking to expand Errin territory, hopefully somewhere without predatory dinosaurs.

Being highly intelligent creatures, boatbuilding had been perused for hundreds of years; the Errin were a seaborne power and amassed their fortunes through exploration and trade up and down the African coast. They were the Neanderthal version of Vikings.

The Errin had developed weapons for defence against the predatory dinosaurs and now also against the slowly encroaching 'Highbrows' (ugly, smaller, densely stupider versions of themselves).

Bows, arrows and throwing spears using short sticks to give the spears more range were the usual for defence, on land and on-board ships. The Draconians on the beach were killed as soon as the bowmen came into range; they then landed and checked out this new type of dinosaur they had discovered.

These new creatures used TOOLS! Dinosaurs using TOOLS! This terrified Keeka. Dinosaurs were bad enough. Intelligent dinosaurs could be catastrophically dangerous, a very bad feeling comes over him. They were almost like people; how could this be? He would need to talk to the wise men and see what they thought; these things could spell the destruction of the Neanderthals.

The Errin had no 'Gods', the concept, totally foreign to them, had never arisen. They did not worship THINGS! They revered knowledge and leadership, so advice would be sought from the clan's brightest and best; they loaded one dinosaur body on board and headed back to their base camp further up the coast.

The whole thing had been seen by a young Draconian hatchling; he scampers back and tells all.

This is the start of the Neanderthal-Draconian War, which eventually causes the extinction of both races.

The War

The war had been raging back and forth for almost one hundred and thirty sun cycles.

It started with small Neanderthal raiding parties destroying one coastal settlement at a time. The locals pleading to their leaders the Koban/Draconians to do something.

They construct coastal defences, sharpened tree trunks embedded in the surf, coils of vines with finger-length thorns stretch across the open beaches, this helps halt the first few raids.

The heavier defences brought a larger fleet to overcome it, and it just spiralled from there; no real winners, just a constant cycle by cycle onslaught.

Hatred drives both species.

With no common language and a complete loathing of each other's appearances, not to mention the Draconians eating the dead and not so dead Neanderthals and the Neanderthals wearing the cured skins of slain Draconians was never going to be a basis for trust or any form of peaceful relations being sought.

Wave upon wave of Neanderthal invasion fleets strike Draconian coastal cities.

Constant sun cycle around attacks, from fleets of ships sent by the Errin to wipe out this much-perceived threat from the obviously intelligent and hated dinosaurs.

And to gain much-needed land for colonisation once the dinosaurs are wiped out.

The Errin would attack coastal villages wiping out all of the inhabitants. Male, female and hatchlings, without mercy or compassion. The hatred for each other was bottomless. The fact that the Draconians had no ocean fleet to retaliate with kept the war going as long as it did.

The Draconians under Koban instruction began fighting back with superior weapons and tactics. Fireworks were turned into weapons, rockets set to explode, and buried mines along the sandy beaches took their toll of invading marauders. Keeka was the first to discover this new tactic.

Ironically after being the first to actually come across the Draconians, Keeka was the first to fall to the new defences.

Keeka, now a seasoned Draconian fighter and on his seventh raid on Draconian soil, led his warriors charging up the beach towards the coastal village they were about to plunder. When all of a sudden, a mighty wind and terrible noise threw him into the air; he landed with a thud onto the sand and tried to immediately rise and charge forward when he noticed his left leg and arm were missing; he could see his leg lying just in front of him, his arm was nowhere in sight.

He could hear and see his warriors flee in panic; he also at last saw his arm. It was being chomped on by a Draconian as it walked down the beach towards him; another lifted his leg, severed just below the knee and started eating that; he was fully conscious as a group of dinosaurs started on him; his screams could be heard well out on the water by the fleeing Neanderthal raiders.

But as in all battles, each side develops strategies to combat each foe's inventions. The war drags on.

The Draconians get regular pauses in the conflict as war-torn invaders leave as supplies and warriors dwindle. There is a space of time before the new force from Errin comes to start the attacks anew. This time is used by the Draconians to bolster defences and try new tactics.

Common practice with the Errin was for the incoming and outgoing fleets to meet off the coast and share hard won intelligence, gained in blood by the retreating often decimated strike force.

The Koban come up with a radical way to fight their opponents.

This came about by a fishing party of Draconians observing a Neanderthal vessel being attacked by a giant squid.

Two Koban try subsuming marine creatures and eventually get themselves shifted into two nine-foot long Plesiosaurs.

It is found when one Koban/Plesiosaur caught up to a much larger squid, he could transform into the larger animal, this was thought to be possible because the squid had no bone mass, so a much larger host could be subsumed; it worked out that a large seven-foot Koban could subsume a squid four times his size.

The first attack of the Koban squid could not have worked out better.

The battle group of newly arrived Errin forces meeting with the retreating savaged units who had fought previously, stopped just in the right place for an attack.

One hundred and fifty-seven Errin boats. Seventy from the retreating war depleted units and eighty-seven new arrivals, fully stocked and loaded with warriors. Fifteen thousand eight hundred and sixty Neanderthal in total were sitting anchored and tied together three miles off the coast. Commanders shuttled from ship-to-ship gleaning information prior to launching their next attack.

The Koban squid waited until nightfall when most of the Neanderthals, bar lookouts were asleep, then they struck.

Two hundred and sixty-seven Koban-controlled squid of various sizes attack the vessels.

Working together, the squid grab one side of each ship and pull them down, over balancing and capsizing the often overloaded, top-heavy vessels. Of the fifteen thousand eight hundred and sixty people on the boats, not one Errin sailor or warrior survives.

This is a great victory, and for the first time, an invasion force has been totally defeated.

With no information getting back to the Errin commanders over the ocean in Erra, no one knew what happened to the task force. The Draconians get some well-needed breathing space before the next assault to plan their next move.

A sun cycle later, three scout ships come creeping in to find out what had happened to their lost fleet; they are not harmed in any way and are allowed to scout along the coast unmolested.

The ships see enough to report back. There is no trace anywhere of the lost fleets. They set off to return to Erra. They do not go home alone.

Gripping the bottom of the boats are thirty smaller Koban/squid, which are now heading to the Errin's mainland.

The Koban are taking the fight to the Errin for the first time. It will finish the war in ways no one could imagine.

On reaching home waters, the scouts rejoice at a perfect, fatality free mission and all bar watch keepers remain on board the three vessels.

The watchmen are all subsumed. The Koban for the first time are in a mammalian life form; it goes well or seems to. The Koban shift from body to body learning as much as possible about their enemy, which they now know are Neanderthals and are called the Errin.

A sun cycle goes by before they can get themselves into the crew of a small war fleet of ships heading back to Draconian waters.

The thirty Koban/Errin are scattered over the ten vessels in the small strike force. On dropping anchor back in Draconian waters, they shift back and kill the crews as they sleep. The Draconians now have a small navy and the personnel who know how to use it, but that's not all they brought back, or left back in Neanderthal-controlled Errin.

The first death from the 'Coughing Sickness', as it comes to be known, comes mere weeks after the Koban had landed in Erra, No one could possibly link the cause.

The first death in Draconia happened three days after the thirty Koban reverted back to Draconian form.

Within days, twenty of the returning Koban/Draconian heroes were dead from massive blood loss as every internal vessel in their bodies burst open. Their eyes ran red with tears of blood.

Back in Erra, within a year the Neanderthal people are gone. No one survives the plague.

By great fortune (for any passing lifeform that is), several active volcanos in the area erupt, the super-hot pyroclastic flows scour the dead cities clean, destroying the pathogen completely.

No evidence that a thriving culture of Neanderthal people was there at all is left for history.

The Draconians suffer a similar fate, only a small portion of the population survive. The Koban are reduced from several thousand to one thousand six hundred and seventy-four.

They leave the surviving Draconians to their fate.

Using the ten ships, the Koban/Draconians split up. Sixty-three Koban to a ship, six hundred and thirty Koban head out to sea. Ten Koban from the original thirty that knew how to sail is on each boat and sees them across the ocean safely. Four ships end up in China. Six head for what will be North Africa passing through a narrow channel into a shallow sea full of islands. Splitting up further, they cover most of what will be Europe; it is one of these groups that finally bump into the Anunnaki.

The other one thousand and forty-four travel up towards the northern end of South America dropping off a few hundred here and there as they travel north. It has been decided that staying in one big group is too dangerous, they revert back to small packs and survive as need be; most move inland following prey animals, it would be a decision that would save their species.

Two sun cycles have passed. The Chinese Koban have entrenched themselves in Chinese myth as 'Sky Dragons' and the 'First Dragon Emperor' and give the Chinese the secret to gunpowder, which sees great use during festivals to their new 'Gods', a concept introduced by the Koban to ensure a more complete rule of their subjects and food source.

The South American Koban have integrated themselves into the Northern South American Indian cultures of the Olmec and Mayan and start up another vast spanning empire securing another productive safe food source, again the new concept of 'Gods' is used to ensure loyalty.

The entire Koban shapeshifting species are now for the most part in human form; with this comes as seen before a susceptibility to human illnesses; care is now kept when dealing with sickness.

The Draconians don't fare as well. Being costal living creatures, they fall foul of a cosmic event.

A large asteroid screams in from deep space and hits the third planet from the sun almost dead centre of the water mass to be later known as the Pacific Ocean.

The impact causes a massive tsunami to form. The wave destroys every coastal area worldwide and is so horrifically remembered as to be seared into every culture's collective memory as 'The Great Flood'.

The Draconians are wiped off the face of the Earth as if they did not exist.

The world spins on. Zin throughout all this time has kept his distance; one hunter against so many is suicide; he occasionally goes into orbit with the shuttle and checks using the shuttle's sensors to see what is going on. The Anunnaki have gone after stripping clean the area of northern Europe they were interested in, so he is back to one foe. Seeing the vast Koban empires, he retreats back into the shadows allowing history to play itself out, but now after seeing the damage caused by the plague and tsunami, he realises the Koban have been hit with their first major blow. Time to see if a further push can be given, he heads to America with the shuttle and settles down in a secluded gully in what will be North American Arizona and starts looking for small groups of Koban to kill.

Present Day Tuba City, Arizona

Zin, now calling himself John Running Fox, has the appearance of a full blood Hopi Indian; he has used this form before so can change into it without having to kill anyone; this particular form had tried to kill him a long time ago. Zin recalls the fierce struggle with the young warrior, Running Fox.

Running Fox had been cast out of the tribe for arguing with the shaman, 'Hunting Dog'. Running Fox had said he had seen the 'Blue Star Kachina', but no one believed him, bar his long-time friend Bright Wing, so Running Fox and Bright Wing went out to find the Blue Star Kachina he saw descend into the dessert. What he actually saw was the failing dropship do its last trip as the ancient technology finally broke down for the last time; the massive bloom of coolant from the damaged engine lighting up the sky with a bright blue flare.

"That's it, Ohna, the old ship is done for. I have just enough lift to put it into that narrow cleft in the side of this hill; we will spend a couple of nights in the ship salvaging whatever we can," says Zin.

"OKAY, SCALEMITE, NOTHING ON SCANS, BUT THERE IS AN INDIAN VILLAGE OVER THE NEXT VALLEY, WE CAN TALK TO THEM AND SEE IF THEY HAVE SEEN ANY KOBAN."

Zin takes everything that is useable and makes up carry harnesses; he is down to one hyper-com unit and a single side arm; all others have been depleted or damaged over the cycles. He calls to Ohna, "Let's go check out the area, we need water and food." With that, he grabs the harness and sets the security measures (explosives set to destroy the shuttle on the opening of the door) and walks towards a stream he had seen. Running Fox and his friend Bright Wing see him leave. Running Fox trails Zin unable from the distance to make out Zin's form, which is still in his natural reptilian state. Bright Wing goes to check out the silvery structure in the cleft. The explosion as he opens the door lights up the valley killing poor Bright Wing and totally destroying the shuttle.

Ohna calls out a warning, "BEHIND YOU, SCALE SCRUBBER!"

The axe which would have cleaved Zin's head wide open glances off his shoulder harness. The Indian screams a war whoop and swings again. Zin, taken by surprise, back pedals and falls on his tail; the Indian immediately dives onto Zin, big mistake! Zin's hand slaps onto the Indian's face; the tendrils in his palms enter skin and paralyses the warrior starting the shift. Thirty beats later, Zin is now Running Fox and has all the skills and language of a Hopi Indian warrior.

For all that, John genuinely liked the Indians and had been with them many times since they came to America from Russia while the land bridge between the continents was still there, simpler times without facial recognition software, passports and such which are now giving him huge problems with travel and transportation.

To deal with the tighter scrutiny, John has money scattered all over the world; gold, diamonds, precious metals and gems and has extensive connections with a variety of underworld criminal sources. When he needs transport, passports, birth certificates, money makes anything possible, private planes and boats are easy to come by.

He is here because of a summons by an old friend, a Hopi medicine man. Now in his nineties who had a strange vision, he wants translated.

He had a vision of a sky person destroying the Hopi nation and it frightened him enough to call out for his adopted son Running Fox. (Spotted Elk had saved John's life years ago after a near miss fighting a group of Koban. Spotted Elk had been fifty-two at the time.)

20th May 1980

After the Mount St Helens explosion, Peter/Zin got a lead on four suspected Koban who had fled from the area heading south; he followed in the jeep; it soon became obvious when they did not stop to sleep that Peter was on the right trail, these were Koban, unknown to Peter/Zin he had been spotted and the Koban were leading him into a trap. After twenty-one hours of nonstop driving bar petrol stops (which may have been when he was spotted), they drive to the Antelope Mesa just above the Hopi reservation. John pulls up and goes over to investigate the stopped car; the four Koban open fire from ambush and Peter is blown off his feet with multiple bullet hits and rolls down a gully, lying prone, his face and body a mass of blood. The Koban seeing this drive away. A Hopi shaman watches from a prayer cave and goes to see what is left of the white man who was shot.

"SCALEMITE, THIS IS WHY I KEEP TELLING YOU TO WEAR THE BULLETPROOF VEST, YOU HAVE A BULLET IN EACH ARM AND ONE GRAZED YOUR SKULL. YOU ARE LOSING QUITE A BIT OF BLOOD SO GET UP AND BACK TO THE CAR." No response from the prone Peter.

At that same moment, Spotted Elk comes down the slope and is stunned to see a six-foot, six-inch tall Kachina Lizard Spirit woman stand over the body.

Sensing a noble spirit and having dealt with Indians in the past, Ohna talks to a startled Spotted Elk.

"I AM A LIZARD KACHINA, PLEASE HELP THIS MAN, HE IS ALSO A KACHINA IN HUMAN FORM."

Spotted Elk still strong even in his early fifties, gets Peter back up to the jeep and drives him to the reservation hospital. Peter recovers and is forever beholden to the old shaman, who after many discussions with Peter/Zin adopts him as his spirit son into the Hopi Indian tribe. Peter had changed into his Hopi form of Running Fox one time to show the shaman his 'true form'.

"I am here, old father, what can you tell me?"

With a croak, the old man starts to speak.

"I am Spotted Elk, hear me. In my vision, I saw the sky turn red, it spat a stone into the Earth; the stone cracked open and grew into a sky beast, hungry enough to eat the world above. Spider Woman came to me. Whispered in my ear to say the beast would grow and give birth too many. Taking the shapes of all the animals, devouring all in their path. Spider Woman said that a great hunter would come and slay the beast bringing peace back to the Hopi. I am Spotted Elk, I have spoken."

"I AM PICKING UP TRACES OF GRAVITOX, VERY FAINT, UNDERGROUND."

"Thank you, old father, we will take a look around the caves and see what can be done."

"HEY, SCALEMITE, YOU LISTENING TO ME?"

The old man nodded almost asleep.

"Go my son, take your Kachina spirit woman and slay the beast."

"WHAT DID HE CALL ME?"

"I will do this thing, with the help of my Kachina lizard goddess." With that, John walked away to get started, but where to look?

"A GODDESS, SEE PEOPLE KNOW MY WORTH UNLIKE SOME SCALE-DIPPED LUMPS I KNOW."

The Gravitox readings were to the east, so John got in the rental car and drove east.

"See if anything shows up on satellite, Ohna."

"OOHHH, GOT A FAINT HEAT BLOOM IN DULCE, NEW MEXICO."

"What's there?"

"ACCORDING TO CONSPIRACY BUFFS, A 'DUMB'?"

"Dumb?"

"DEEP UNDERGROUND MILITARY BASE."

"Worth a look, it's a six-hour drive, let's head out, we will gas up en route and grab something to eat, let's see what we find in the morning."

Pentagon E Ring

"HE SAID WHAT!" spluttered the general's aide.

"He said for a price he can offer the United States Government the ability for people to live extended lives, to be virtually immortal; he gave a ream of scientific formula and said to show it to any competent scientist. We did! And it checks out!"

"Holy shit! Put me through to the general."

The general was Thomas Drake, he was the president's national security advisor, and close friend to the man who was getting old and frail with many lingering health issues.

"General Drake, you won't believe this!" The general is briefed by the aide.

"So let me get this straight, for the use of the Dulce Deep Underground Military Base they will give us this 'eternity drug', thing! What's the catch? There is no such thing as a free lunch as the old saying goes," says Drake with more than a hint of sarcasm.

"That's what they said, sir. They also asked for a meeting, somewhere remote. They want to send someone to talk directly with you, weird request was your height and weight, we think it is probably for identification purposes," says the aide with a shrug.

"Set it up, the quicker the better," General Drake replies with a frown.

It was arranged for the following week. Three days away.

The meeting was set up in a modest hotel, 'The Springs Resort'. Thirty-seven miles from Dulce base, security checked the hotel and grounds; they even had frogmen check the pond in front of the hotel; all was in order.

General Drake walked into the meeting, but it wasn't General Drake that walked out, the Koban Alpha male Gnaff saw to that.

The Koban had reverted back to a long tried and tested method ensuring they could flourish, get inside and take control.

This idea had come from studying the humans for centuries, who for some weird reason would believe nearly anything put to them in certain ways.

Belief of country, religion, money, power and of course the chance of everlasting life.

The Koban exploited all of these things and had been doing so for millennia. People would do anything just for the promise of everlasting life.

The Koban introduced cults with charismatic leaders who could gather thousands of people.

Early man worshiping snakes.

The Mayans with their jaguar cult.

Egyptians using a mass of gods all demanding sacrifice and offering everlasting life.

All a con! Courtesy of the Koban.

Modern humans were not 'quite' so gullible, but even nowadays cults thrive, preying on simple, vulnerable people or people who would not be missed.

Most missing people all over the country are not even searched for.

America alone has one hundred thousand people go missing each year.

Underground bases around the country controlled by the bogus Colonel Drake would become processing plants to feed the Koban using the missing people and cult followers as food stock.

John Running Fox entered the Dulce area just as General Drake was inspecting the base deep underneath Archuleta Mesa.

Drake/Gnaff loved what he was seeing. The perfect secure, secret, manageable base that the sixteen Koban left in

America, after the alpha female left the planet with the Mount St. Helens blast could exploit. The Koban Colonel Drake using his rank and friendship with the president began making changes to Dulce Base. The first three floors were pure military and acted as a smoke screen.

The floors four down to seven were something else entirely.

Unmarked black military helicopters brought people to the base in a constant stream. Hundreds of them. In complete secrecy. Compartmentalised, so secret. No one knew what was happening, but hundreds went in…not one came out.

The local Indians were the first to notice something was off about the mesa.

The Jicarilla Apache were a fiercely proud people, so when tribe members went missing, they went looking. What they uncover is horrifying.

Dulce Base, New Mexico

Donald Firemaker, Apache Indian from the Jicarilla reservation, had been a security guard at Dulce Base for five years, good steady work, better than the casino's, with very little grief and no need to do the Indian act for the N-daa white eyes. Other than the occasional conspiracy nut trying to get in to find aliens…Aliens!…Little green men for Christ's sake!…The jokes in the ready room were funny as hell; they even had a picture of ET phoning home, some clever wit had written reverse the charges underneath, but lately, some seriously weird shit has been happening.

Firemaker was only cleared to go to Level 3.

His pass card for the freight elevator only allowed the keys to Level 3 to work.

He had been complaining for weeks his card was faulty, but would they listen…OH, NO!

Donald Firemaker, clipboard in hand, stepped into the elevator, slid his card into the slot, pressed button three and got a mild electric shock for his trouble.

"Bastard card."

Rubbing his fingers, he watched the floor indicator lights blink on 01, 02, 03, 04.

"What the fu—?"

05. "Shit."

06. "FUCK!"

07. The door slid open to hell on earth…Firemaker backed up until he was pressed hard against the back wall of the elevator and started screaming.

The doors opened into a vast open chamber, natural stone walls, high ceiling, diffused muted lights making it difficult to see the far wall.

Firemaker stood rigid with fright still pressing himself back against the far wall of the freight elevator watching a seven-foot-tall, human-shaped reptile eat the face off a screaming totally naked Indian male.

His screams stopped! Firemaker's just got louder.

The lift doors closed and started back up. On Level 1, they found Firemaker on the floor of the lift sobbing.

Security colleagues shouting questions of what happened finally take him to the medical wing where a paramedic is forced to give him a sedative; he is then wheeled away to a medical room.

Firemaker comes around strapped to a medical gurney.

He is confused, totally naked and back in the freight elevator, out the corner of his eye he sees the lights, 05. 06. He starts screaming again. 07.

The doors open, two fully dressed soldiers in full battle rig unstrap him and push him through a door into a rough-walled cell, inside are six more naked men all native Apache Indians.

"Welcome to the underworld, brother," said the oldest. "It is a good day to die."

Jicarilla Apache Reservation

"Welcome to the Jicarilla Apache Reservation, cousin, we got a call from Spotted Elk, he talks highly of you and your spirit guide, Lizard woman. I am George Norroso."

Striding forward, he takes John's hand in a firm grip, telling of the great strength he had had as a younger man.

"Spotted Elk spoke highly of your wisdom and power as a shaman of the Apache people, hopefully we can aid each other," John said with a nod of his head in respect to the old shaman.

"There is much evil in the Archuleta Mesa, we have many men and women missing from the area, plus we are hearing of many missing homeless people in the surrounding townships. The Kachinas are angry, we must find what is required to appease the spirits."

Shaking his head while one hand grasped a leather pouch on a lanyard containing charms, the old shaman looks into John's eyes. "Help us."

"We will, can you get me as much information as possible about the base and any secret entrances your people have to get into the mountain?"

"Yes, leave me to get it done. Someone will meet you at your hotel, a room is waiting for your use."

The old shaman goes over to his desk, sits down and starts making phone calls.

Three men and one woman come into John's room later that day, the men were all tall, lean and hard looking, the woman was a strikingly beautiful Apache maiden (she reminded him of an Apache woman he met a long time ago called Liluye or 'Hawk Singing'). The woman made the introductions.

"Hi, I am Grace Imala, to your right is Ira Tarak, centre is Caleb Elan and over by the wall, that's Billy Cochise." All three men nod as their names are spoken.

"We have detailed plans of the base and several local entrances to sacred prayer caves along the mesa that the shamans use; they have told us of frightening noises from some air vents, and locals have seen spirits running on the plain. Lizard Kachinas. We do not know for sure if our people are in there, but if they are, it will be in the very bowels of the base. The underworld."

"Let's see the plans and try to work out how we get in and check what's there." John walks over to the table as Grace spreads out the maps, she brought in.

"Where does this prayer cave lead to? It looks like it goes straight into the centre of the Mesa." John points to a section on the map. "Looks good, let's go have a look." He turns to see four terrified stares in return. "What?"

All four at the same time cry out, "NO, no, not there! It's haunted by really evil spirits; we cannot go in." Four pale faces nod in unison.

"Fine, take me there I will go look myself." And with a smile, he says, "I have my own Kachina spirit to protect me."

"DAMN RIGHT, SCALEMITE, LET'S GO STAND ON SOME TAILS."

Archuleta Mesa (Dulce Base)

The spirit cave was so well hidden he would never have found it without the aid of the Apache. Saying a farewell, John heads into the cave; the three men armed with rifles scatter around the entrance to cover it; the woman comes into the cave, pulling out a massive handgun. She nods to John and settles into a corner of the cave to wait. With a nod, John heads down the shallow downward slope. With his light sensitive eyes, John can see quite well in the darkness of the cave. Bioluminescent moss glows softly on the walls in patches helping him manoeuvre easily; he picks up the pace.

"GRRRRRAAAARG!" John stops! Stone still.

"WE HAVE A SHAPESHIFTER 200 YARDS TO OUR FRONT," Ohna calls quietly.

"No shit, Sherlock!" John stands still, a slight breeze is felt on his face bringing with it the smell of death. "It can't smell us? The air is being forced out of the cave somehow? We go in slow and steady."

"SHIFT TO A VELOCIRAPTOR, YOU HAVE BEFORE, USE THE THIRTY BEATS NOW WHILE IT IS SAFE."

"Good idea, Ohna, here goes."

Stripped naked, John's form begins to blur then just like the special effects in 'American Werewolf in London', his face expands to become a muzzle full of teeth, a tail appears, scales and strong claw-tipped feet and hands, finally thirty seconds or beats later stood a six-and-a-half-foot tall Velociraptor.

"YOU LOOK GREAT BACK IN SCALES, NO MITES, MIND, GIVE ME A TWIRL, OOOOH, NICE."

"Quiet, let's go."

Claw tips click as John the Velociraptor slinks down the tunnel. Just ahead hunched over a definitely dead half eaten naked human is a Koban in Draconian form, next to no muzzle, very human-looking face but with rows of small, sharp, serrated teeth, which were busy tearing the muscle from the victim's shoulder.

John the Velociraptor springs forward, the vicious extended hooked claws on the feet not designed as the movies show to disembowel but more like a lions to grab and hold; it is the powerful jaws that do the damage, locking onto the throat of the Koban youth tearing it out completely, blood spraying everywhere. It is over in seconds, silently.

"WHAT'S IT TASTE LIKE? IS IT LIKE DURGO? ARE YOU GOING TO EAT IT OR WHAT? GET ITS BRAINS, THEY MUST TASTE GREAT. IS IT LIKE DURGO…OKAY, SORRY, YOU CAN'T TALK WITH YOUR MOUTH FULL. OOOO, LOOK IT'S GOT SCALEMITES!" Giggle and farts of laughter.

"Don't even joke about something like that, ARRRG, THE TWO HELLS."

"TOLD YOU…SCALEMITES." Loud continuous giggles.

John in Velociraptor form quickly checks the entire cavern scratching all the way, no more Koban, plenty of bodies though. John shifts back and dresses then heads for the surface, still absently scratching one arm.

"THE SCALEMITES DID NOT TRANSFER, YOU ARE CLEAN, MIGHTY SCALEMITE DESTROYER."

"DURGO…It tastes just like Durgo…who would have thought."

"I MISS EATING," moans Ohna.

"Right, let's get the others and see what else we can eat, sorry see."

"SCALE-ROTTED FUNGAL-INFESTED DURGO DROPPINGS," grumbles a frustrated Ohna.

John laid out what he had found, but not the method of doing so. They decide to try one more site, one that even the holiest of shaman feared to go.

"PICKING UP GRAVITOX READINGS, VERY SMALL BUT IT'S THERE, DEFINITE KOBAN PRESENCE. TAKE A PRISONER THIS TIME, LET'S GET SOME INFORMATION ON NUMBERS AT LEAST. DON'T EAT ANYTHING WITHOUT TELLING ME ALL THE JUICY DETAILS...OKAY?"

"Okay." John looks at the four humans. "Same as the last time, guys, guard my back and I will go in; this time, I might be a while." With that, John runs into the cave, going far enough in so he could not be seen; he strips off in preparation for the shift, thirty beats later and John the Velociraptor is charging down the tunnel.

"YOU LOOK SO SEXY AS A VELOCIRAPTOR...GRRRRRR."

"By the serpent, Ohna, give it a rest. I have not had any couplings for millennia."

"WHAT ABOUT ALL THE HUMANS YOU HAVE HUMP..."

"Quiet! I hear something."

Sneaking up to a corner in the tunnel, he lays flat and looks around the stonewall. There are several chained humans sitting in a group, all Apache Indians, standing over them are three reptilian Koban juveniles; they are arguing with each other, hands moving up and down, using what can only be described as their version of rock, paper, scissors to decide the winner. The winner stands to the side and the other two head for a door in the far wall. The winner rears back his head and lets out a victorious 'GGRRRRRRAAAG!' The humans start to wail.

One human is selected, unlocked from the chain and virtually thrown across the floor; he gets up and starts to run. So, this was to be a feeding ritual with a chase and kill, very common on all shapeshifter worlds. John gets ready to pounce.

"HUMPED! REMEMBER THE SCALEMITES?"

John waited until the human ran towards the tunnel he was in, allowed him to pass then hit the charging Koban with a head-butt, knocking the creature unconscious. Dragging the Koban by its left foot, he strides over to the chained prisoners, who all started screaming and struggling with the chains. Well, a movie-size Velociraptor would do that to you, and all of them had seen *Jurassic Park* of course, so when it spoke to them in their own language that was the last straw.

"Brothers, I am a Kachina spirit. I am here to set you free. Go! Your sister and brothers are in the world above…go."

Breaking the chain was easy, seven Apache men ran for their lives back up the tunnel…using the same chain, he secures the now conscious Koban.

"Now let's have a chat, what language would you prefer? I know many."

With that, he bites off the Koban's left foot…screams filled the chamber.

"How many are there of you here?"

A shake of the head, crunch, another bite to just below the knee.

"S-s-sixteen, t-there a-are s-sixteen of us," stammers the Koban/Draconian.

"Good, tell me more before I start getting peckish."

After only a couple more bites costing the Koban its entire left leg and John knew everything about the Koban plan for Earth, or as much as this youngster knew, the last bite took its head, and as Ohna said, the brains are delicious.

Returned to his human form, John joins the Indians on the surface, where wild stories are flying between the freed men and their rescuers.

"IT WAS A FUCKING VELOCIRAPTOR! RIGHT OUT OF FUCKING JURASSIC PARK!" screams Donald Firemaker. Then in a softer voice almost a whisper he says, "It spoke to us."

The others murmur their agreement. The mountains were a holy place to the Indians and strange things were common place, this would need discussing with the tribe's holy men. The shamans would tell them what to do. The small group of Indians plus John make their way back to the reservation, plans need to be made to cleanse the mountain. Underneath the mountain, other discoveries were being made.

A Koban alpha's challenge roar fills the chamber.

"GGGGRRRRAAAACKKKKKKKK! What has happened?"

An angry Colonel Drake strides back and forth before his assembled younger siblings, all are in Koban/Draconian form. Drake's tail is a blur going side to side.

"Zonti, Dobux, both dead…DEAD! How can these weak creatures kill one of us down here? They have no claws or teeth; they had no weapons; our brother's blood was all that was found."

Stopping dead still, he looks at the assembled Koban and with a slow hiss says, "Search this place, find out what happened, gather all the humans in the lowest chamber and guard them well; we will have a feast to the fallen when we find out what is happening here. NOW GO!"

Jicarilla Reservation

John and the others returned to the reservation and were now in a council of war. With the help of Donald Firemaker, they had full plans of the facility and a pass card, which may or may not get them to Level 07. After taking in police reports, missing persons and general hearsay, the group thinks there are at least forty-six Apache people and maybe seventy others held in the underground base. Using the shaman's knowledge of the prayer caves, several groups of Apaches will try and rescue the captives. John and Donald Firemaker will go in through the front door and take out the leader, Colonel Drake.

There are eight prayer caves. The Apache send five-man groups down into each one. All well-armed with semi-automatic weapons, every group has one man with a pump action shotgun for close in work, and every man also carries a handgun, a knife and/or tomahawk.

John and Donald Firemaker go in the front gate dressed as guards; by coincidence, John looks like one of the other Apache guards, so now has his ID card and swipe card. John and Donald start the shift and patrol the corridors as normal, blending into the background. Over the tanoy, they hear, "Colonel Drake, please report to the roof helipad, your helicopter has just landed." John and Donald share a look…their target is gone.

All the Apache groups head into the caves, headlamp torches light the way; they make quick time down into the bowels of the mountain. It is in the end an anti-climax. All of the groups come across single or small groups of two or three

Koban and shoot them dead; they are as easy to kill as any human. All in all, they kill twelve of the Koban.

Drake and his aide Burex in the form of Major Linus O'Tool get away. All of the prisoners are freed unharmed. The base is completely unaware anything has occurred beneath their feet, only the special security squad of thirty men, all under the thrall of the Koban, know something is amiss. Lieutenant Franks calls the colonel with the news of the attack, he has to hold the phone away from his ear! The scream could be heard across the room.

"Find out who these men were? I want names. I WANT VENGEANCE! I WANT BLOOOOD!!!PILOT! New course, take us to the White House."

There had been rumours for years, conspiracy nut stuff, science fiction films, all sorts of shit. 'The Reptilians in the White House'. David Ike started it years ago. And now, his understudy Tom Marks has taken it even further, openly spouting his theories to any who would listen…WELL! It's all true!

Colonel Drake/Gnaff and Major O'Tool/Burex are escorted to the vice president's office. Inside the closed room, they both bow deep before the alpha female Koban who is in the form of a stunningly beautiful human female. Six feet tall, Nordic-looking, piercing ice-blue eyes, pale blonde hair. Her name is Flinexa, but in this human form, it is Erika Brynja; she walks around the desk, hands on hips, and hisses.

"What in the hells brings you here? Especially at this time, we are close, very close…REPORT NOW!"

Both males drop to their knees trembling, the burst of pheromones from the alpha female overpowering them.

"We are still awaiting reports from our human slaves, but I think the hunter is on our tracks."

Another blast of pheromones.

"OF COURSE, IT'S THE HELL'S BLASTED HUNTER, WHO ELSE COULD IT BE? YOU IDIOT! YOU WILL GO BACK AND KILL THIS PIECE OF GONGO EXCREMENT. NOW!"

Both men crawl towards the door, come to their feet and scurry out the office, and as they leave, her aide pops his head around the door; he is a human thrall or slave.

"Madam Vice President, do you still want that restraint order on Tom Marks?"

"Yes, he knows too much, see it's done soon, we are too close to completing this phase."

The aide quietly closes the door and walks over to his desk and starts making phone calls.

Erika Brynja/Flinexa reaches into a special drawer and grabs a squealing, hairless rat. Reverts to her Draconian form, which only takes ten seconds in her case. Her reptilian form emerges. Teal green scales, bright orange frill, a completely removed tail done years earlier to making blending into humanity easier, the almost human-shaped face and body does not require the removal of clothing, the rat disappears in one gulp; she always eats when stressed. Shaking her head, she grabs another rat…it has been a stressful time, she is one week away from being crowned president of the United States. Then the complete subjugation of this world could be realised. Her mother had left them an amazing constantly refilling food store…She would be in complete control of it, no more hiding in this horrible pale skin. She remembers a time long ago when they all walked among the food stock as GODS.

BREAKING NEWS, BREAKING NEWS flashed across TV screens everywhere in the world. US PRESIDENT, ALEX MANDEL IS DEAD. AFTER A LONG FIGHT WITH CANCER, THE 68-YEAR-OLD PRESIDENT MANDLE DIED AT 4:37 THIS MORNING. A STATEMENT WILL BE GIVEN FROM THE WHITE HOUSE LATER TODAY.

"EXCELLENT." The vice president smiled smugly. Soon to be sworn in President Erika Brynja swings back and forth in her plush seat behind her desk; her tail may be gone, but the habit was still there.

Apache Reservation, New Mexico

In the aftermath of the raid, all the surviving Apache people went back to families and friends; the others, all mostly youngish men (more meat on a male torso), wanted revenge; all were either down and outs or criminals; nobody had even looked for these people. John offered them a deal, revenge and a chance of money, lots of money. He has done this before many times to garner support. The Koban need money to buy or bribe for power; there will be a secret stash in the mountain. This was the lure he used to recruit his strike team.

Willie Hawkins and Jake Lincon

Both men had been friends for a great number of years and had been living off the streets since their medical discharge from the Marines in 2005. Willie and Jake had been a sniper team, Willie was the spotter and Jake was the trigger man. They were inseparable and usually got some heavy-duty jokes from their Marine buddies about being gay, or at least being very happy with each other.

Operation 'Outlaw Destroyer' was a counterinsurgency operation to stop weapons and bomb-making efforts in Tikrit, Iraq.

Sniper Team 'Viper' (Willie and Jake) had set up as overwatch protecting a Marine foot patrol doing house-to-house searches.

Right from the start, everything went wrong. Their Iraqi guide was working with the rebels so the whole thing was a set-up.

Willie and Jake were taken on the roof as they lay behind the 50 cal. Barret and targeting scope; they never had a chance.

Tied up and left on the roof in their sniper's perch, they had a grandstand view of the foot patrol being wiped out by automatic AK-47 gunfire below them.

Willie and Jake are horrendously tortured over the next four days and are due to be decapitated live and in full colour on Al Jazeera TV at 8 pm on the fifth day of their capture.

In a textbook perfect rescue, a SEAL team gets them out right in the middle of the Al Jazeera recording.

Seal Team 3

Two officers, one chief, and thirteen SEALs head for a remote corner of Takrit, Iraq, in a Blackhawk helicopter with an Apache gunship as overwatch; all the men are highly trained, fully briefed and ready to get the job done. This would be an insertion by rope onto the flat roof of the suspected building, the chopper would then circle around and land in the walled courtyard; by that time if the planning stays on track and 'Murphy' does not mess it up too much, they should be wheels up again in ten minutes. It goes like clockwork.

The chief and eight men rope down onto the roof and stack by the roof top door. The two officers and the five remaining guys, two being medics, debus the chopper as it lands and go in through the metal rear door into the house. Flashbangs from above and below totally disorientate the rebels. The two Marines are on their knees on the floor and drop on their faces as soon as the first flashbang goes off, with less likelihood now of a 'blue on blue', the SEALs kill all of the standing targets. Three round bursts into faces and chests eliminates the twenty-seven rebels who are in the house. The whole thing is over in just three minutes. Willie and Jake are hustled out and given over to the medics, all board the idling Blackhawk and are soon airborne and headed to the nearest American safe area, not one SEAL has made a single noise, all silently leave the chopper each giving Willie and Jake a squeeze or tap on their shoulders as they pass, tears stream down both Marines' faces as reality hits them. Safe!

They are sent home to recover, they never do.

Drink and drugs to block the pain and memories soon sees them discharged from the Marines in 2005. They end up living off the streets, eventually ending up in New Mexico and being captured by the Koban to end up in Dulce Base as food stock.

White House Oval Office

"I do solemnly swear that I will faithfully execute the office of president of the United States and will, to the best of my ability, preserve, protect, and defend the constitution of the United States."

With this short sentence, Erika Brynja became the first female president of the United States of America. Around the world, people were either pleased, displeased or, as the majority of them, could not care less. A small group however was celebrating the coming of the new age of the Koban on Earth. All one hundred and twenty-three of them.

The original mother had lain thousands of eggs, all had now hatched and were almost fully mature; only a fully mature and strong female could leave a planet. The burst of power on ejection from the planet catalysed the sperm stored over years in the alpha female and fertilises her eggs. The female then goes dormant until a suitable planet is sensed, then the pod hits the planet, burrows in and the cycle starts again.

Flinexa/Erika Brynja can feel her power increase, she is near time to becoming a mother; soon she will leave this place to her siblings, as long as the planet survives her explosive exit that is. She has already found an underground power source. A geothermal tap directly to the planet's mantel in a place called Yellowstone National Park. With more than enough stored power to expel her into the vastness of space.

Dulce Base Archuleta Mesa New Mexico

John, Donald Firemaker and the thirty-five survivors who chose to go back into the base, sprint down the familiar tunnels into the lower levels of the base. All are armed with modern weapons and body armour, Kevlar helmets with built-in lamps light the way ahead. Firemaker has given them as much information as possible plus what John got out of the Koban he killed, tells them what they are about to face.

"There are forty-three security personnel in total, it breaks down to nine monitoring staff, one team leader, a lieutenant and a platoon of thirty-three well-trained troopers; we will have to take out the platoon. Good news is they are arrogant and lazy, due to being nothing but prison guards for so long, but their training will kick in pretty quick, so we have to take out as many by surprise as possible; this is how we will do it," John said.

They split into three groups, John leading one with sixteen men, Firemaker with another sixteen fighters. The last three guys are left as rear guard and medical support.

They advance down the two chosen tunnels in complete darkness, just before they hit the large caverns which are lit by overhead strip lights, all switch off their night vision goggles (NVGs). Each man has flash bang grenades on their harnesses, these will be the element of surprise John is looking for. Well-trained men tend to do specific things under specific conditions, John is going to exploit that.

Talking into his mic, John calls the strike force, "Ready on my mark."

Two men, Willie and Jake, the team's snipers and snoopers, had crawled into the cavern beforehand and were at the power box controlling the lights in both caverns.

"Ready, guys! Blow the lights."

A loud pop is heard! Then total darkness. A screaming voice from one of the guard's shouting.

"GO TO NVGs!" is heard. Standard Operating Procedure (SOPs). Just as John had predicted.

"Ready! Throw flash bangs in…three, two, one!"

John following his own orders, pulls the pin from the cylindrical grenade and tosses it into the cavern, closing his eyes and covering his ears at the same time.

Multiple loud booms and bright strobes of light fill the chamber.

"Goggles on! Kill everyone not wearing green!" screams John.

All his people had bright green flouro scarfs around their necks.

Pops of rifle fire fill the caverns. The security troops are caught flat-footed, disorientated and blind.

It is more like an execution than a firefight.

None of the thirty-three security troops survive. Sadly, four of Firemaker's guys are killed, by, if you can call it that, 'friendly fire'.

John's men only suffer a couple of small wounds caused by flying stone shards. With the underground level taken, the medics patch up the wounded and place the fallen to the side for later retrieval.

They head up to take the rest of the base. Well, the levels below Level 03 that is.

Above in Level 03, the soldiers and staff are totally oblivious to the raging battle below their feet.

They regroup at the Level 07 stairwell and go over the next phase of battle.

"Okay, that went well, we only have nine bad guys to worry about now, and according to the Koban I talked to said there are security block houses on each floor, so it should be three guys in each. We will approach with stealth. Toss in flash bangs then rush the door and take out the guys inside!

Everybody good?" John looks around and gets multiple nods from the strike team. "Let's go then."

They slink up the spiral stairway two men at a time, soft shoe quiet, a quick peek around the last bend shows a wide cut stone chamber with the security room in the form of a porta-cabin directly across from the freight elevator and next to the stairway leading up to Level 05. A large '06' is painted on the wall and a smaller '06' is on the freight elevator.

A large glass window in the front of the security station showed one guy sitting at a desk. No sign of anyone else from the view they had.

John draws out his handgun, a Berretta 92 and screws on a silencer. He slides along the wall towards the door facing him, two of his men Willie and Jake cover him with raised rifles, seconds later, which felt like hours, he is at the door.

"SCALEMITE, THERE ARE FOUR HEAT BLOOMS. I CAN SENSE TWO OF THEM ARE LOWER TEMPERATURE. THESE MAY BE DORMANT, TAKE CARE, MY SCALE SCRUBBER."

Flattened against the door, John waves over one of the strike team men. Duke Geneva is a huge former gangland enforcer from New York and built like the proverbial stone-pooping place.

"On my word, Duke, hit the door." John grips the gun and nods to Duke. "…NOW!"

BANG! The door slams against the wall. John steps in and…POP-POP-POP-POP! Four dead guards lie on the floor, all shot in the head, two had been asleep on chairs.

"Great shooting, boss, that was class." He nods his head in professional approval.

"Thanks, Duke, years and years of practice."

The group now head up to Level 05. As they get to the corner, they can hear voices and a strange scuffing sound, a quick look around the corner sees two men drag a round, matt, green, bulky 'something' out of the elevator. A single guard can be seen sitting at the security station window staring at a screen, John has a weird feeling about the bulky-looking round thing.

"DROP SCALE SCUFFER! IT IS A ROBOTIC SENTRY GUN! I CAN SENSE IT LOCKING ON TO HEAT SOURCES FROM THE GROUP."

Unknown to the invaders, they had tripped a laser security beam on Level 07. The guards knew they were coming; the two operators drag the weapon clear of the elevator, hit the button bringing the sentry gun on-line, and anything in front of it was now a target for the 30cal rotary gatling gun. A ripping noise fills the air and all hell breaks loose.

PRRRRRRRRAPPPPPPP! Tracer fire tears down the stone corridor ricocheting off walls, tearing through two, three men at a time! Chunks of flesh fly off, blood mists the air, screams fill the tight space, and with no cover other than a comrade's body, the group gets decimated.

John shifts. Lying flat, he changes into a long lean Sabre-toothed tiger, thirty seconds later and the change is complete, just as the automatic gun shudders to a halt. Its ammunition depleted.

As the two men behind it start to change the ammo magazine, John strikes.

Leaping off the floor in one bound, he lands between the two men.

He literally rips them to pieces, arms, legs, guts, heads…blood flies everywhere. Just at that, the guard inside comes out to help. John takes his head clean off with one bite.

"EEEEWW, YUCK! NEVER LIKED YOU ALL HAIRY LIKE THAT. CHANGE BACK QUICK, OOH YUCK, YOU ARE COVERED IN THAT GUY'S…EYUUUG! CHANGE QUICK."

Thirty beats later and a naked John goes to check his men. Three survivors, no wounded, he just stands shaking his head. "You guys okay?" Willie and Jake nod, shaken to the core. Big Duke just shrugs and shakes his head.

"GET GEAR AND CLOTHES, SCALEMITE, IT'S NOT LIKE YOU HAVE NOT BEEN HERE BEFORE. REMEMBER THE SPARTANS. I LIKED THE SPARTANS. WE SHOULD GO CHECK THEM OUT AGAIN, AT LEAST LET'S SEE THE FILM AGAIN. 'THIS IS SPARTA!' CAN WE? CAN WE? CAN WE?"

"TWO HELLS, OHNA, YOU HAVE NO RESPECT."

"MY JOB IS TO KEEP YOU SAFE AND AS SANE AS YOUR LITTLE SCALEMITE-INFECTED BRAIN CAN BE. SO, TOUGHEN UP AND GET DRESSED, AVENGE YOUR SOFTSKINS AND KILL THE SCALE-DIPPED KOBAN."

Talking to a still shaken Willie and Jake, and stone-cold calm Duke, John says, "Okay! There are two left. Probably the leader and his bodyguard or assistant, let's finish this."

"SCALEMITE! INTERROGATE THE LEADER, WE NEED MORE INFORMATION."

"I was going to. He will tell me everything," was the cold chilling reply from John.

"THAT'S MY SCALE CLEANER, LET'S GO."

Fully dressed and armed in bloody but serviceable battle gear, John heads up to Level 04, this will be an administration and maybe a barracks area? He has no real idea. At the final turn, he sees the security station, it seems unmanned; he slinks along the wall and peeks into the room through the window…empty. He is just turning to go when the elevator pings its arrival. John ducks into the empty station, Willie, Duke and Jake right behind him. The lift doors open to reveal the lieutenant and a corporal whose arms are filled with documents and folders; they virtually walk right into John's hands.

"THAT'S LUCKY, SCALEMITE…GET THEM, BITE THE HEAD OFF THE LITTLE ONE. OKAY, FORGET THAT YOUR LITTLE HUMAN MOUTH WOULD NOT BE UP TO IT, SHOOT HIM INSTEAD."

"Two hells, Ohna, be quiet." John brings up his handgun and says, "FREEZE."

Both men do just that, the lieutenant starts to bawl and shout, "What the hell is going on here?" The corporal's eyes don't leave the barrel of the new gun John had picked up. The gun barrel's bore looks big enough to crawl into, a .45 does that to you. Willie, Jake, and Duke take up positions outside keeping watch.

"SHUT UP, LIEUTENANT! Corporal, tie the lieutenant to that chair, use the duct tape on the shelf, arms and legs if you please."

The non-com did just that, and with no need to check for sloppy knots, the lieutenant was secure.

"Sit down, corporal, use the duct tape to do both your legs and one arm. I will get the rest."

The man did as he was told and with a couple of quick turns of duct tape, both were secure.

"Now let's have a little chat."

"MY TURN, SCALE SCRUBBER!"

With a slight pop, Ohna's avatar appears in the room.

A nearly seven-foot tall, pissed-off-looking, two-legged dinosaur. With a face full of large pointed teeth.

Ohna lets out a great ripping roar!

Both men shit themselves. In the corporal's case literally, the smell fills the room, both men strain against the duct tape but to no avail; the corporal passes out; Ohna brings her snout down near the petrified lieutenant's face.

"WE READY TO TALK NOW?"

Nods come from the sweating man as a dark stain covers the front of his combat pants.

"OOOOOH, THAT WAS SO MUCH FUN."

John opens the door and pretends to let Ohna out, she disappears. Three wide-eyed men look in, John nods over. "I will explain later." He gets worried nods in return from his three remaining men.

"Okay! Let's talk."

He gets it all, the president, the military, the processing plants, the missing hundreds of thousands…Everything!

How to stop it would be something else altogether. Then he remembers a similar situation years ago, what was that scale ticks name again?

"Oh yes. PoNgbe or his Koban name Turen. He and his clutch of Koban sure did a number on the poor Olmec."

South Central Mexico, 3000 Years Ago

The clutch of eggs that had hatched in the large southern continent had flourished and were now fairly strong juveniles, as per usual alpha females and males had taken charge of the group.

They had eaten their way up and down the coastal side of the landmass from what would be called Guatemala, El Salvador, Costa Rica, Panama and back up again.

The upright-walking hairless primates always gave them the best value, they tasted great for one and were easily manipulated into thinking the shapeshifters to be 'GODS'.

The Koban loved to be served and the local natives did this with a passion, nothing was too much to appease their 'GODS'…nothing.

The Koban were past masters at manipulation, but eventually, they would get to a point where their subjects would rebel and force them to flee; with so few numbers and having the physical weakness of whatever they shifted into, they were vulnerable to mass attacks by aggrieved former subjects; they had to know when to cut and run.

Of the original twenty-three in their clutch, only fifteen of them were now left alive, several had been killed by forest animals and angry tribes people over the years, and with no way of reproducing until fully mature, the fifteen that were left were the most devious, downright evil of them all, and look, they may have just hit pay dirt.

The Olmec tribe was about three hundred and fifty people strong; the information they had gotten from other tribes described them as stupid, backward and very superstitious. The very thing they had been looking for.

The Koban would make them strong and successful through manipulation, magic tricks, cons and of course, real 'LIVE GODS' to worship and serve.

It works so well they end up staying with the Olmec's for centuries, making them the most powerful natives in the area…but at a cost, ooooh, such a cost.

The Olmec King or 'TU' was called PoNgbe. He was a giant of a man in height and girth, with the flat low-browed face and squashed nose common to his people.

The alpha Koban male Turen ambushed PoNgbe while he was sleeping in his hut; he never felt a thing as Turen subsumed his body shifting into an exact replica of PoNgbe.

Bu the shaman of transformations was taken by the alpha Koban female Kivex. The other elites of the Olmec clan, Keli, Bada, Tali, Tutu and Yope all went the same way, subsumed by members of the small Koban group.

The next day was to be a revelation for the simple Olmec people.

The gods they had been told about for years but had never seen, and truth be known, no one really cared about too much, were about to make an appearance. 'Live and in the flesh'.

"OLMECS, HEAR ME!" cried PoNgbe/Tureen. "I AM SUMMONING THE GODS TO COME TO US!"

He lifts his arms up to the sky. "TO LIVE WITH US!"

He wraps his beefy arms around his chest. "TO PROTECT US."

"Shaman Bu! (Shaman Bu was 'supposed' to be the transformation shaman up until now that was just talk, now it was reality) bring forth the WERE-JAGUAR."

This was a revered but feared Olmec deity, a human/jaguar hybrid. Into the light walks a very large black jaguar.

All the crowd gasp and take a step back. The jaguar transforms into the native elite Keli…OOOOS cry out from the crowd.

"Shaman Bu, bring forth the Sky Dragon."

Out walks the Koban Vixan in the form of a six-foot Draconian. OOOOOs and AAAAHHs.

"Shaman Bu, send out the Thunder Lizard."

The Koban Bunix walks out in the form of a seven-foot high Velociraptor. Claps and cries of joy fill the air.

"Shaman Bu, send forth the protector twins."

Koban pair Sizzen and Divexx appear as two giant heavily muscled Olmec warriors who used to be the elites Tutu and Yope of the Olmec tribe.

"OLMECS, WE ARE YOUR LEADERS AND GODS, WE WILL MAKE YOU STRONG AND FEARED THROUGHOUT THE LANDS, LET US HAVE A HOLY FEAST TO CELEBRATE THIS DAY. BOW DOWN TO YOUR GODS."

Every Olmec young and old fell to their faces, and on a word of command, a great feast was started; it took two days before the merriment came to a halt, the people were ecstatic. With gods at their side, they would be invincible.

The first to feel the wrath of the Olmec was a neighbouring village that had treated them badly, mocking them, calling names, making fun. The entire village was lain to waste two hundred people killed or captured.

A new demand from the Koban GODS. The captured were to be sacrificed to them.

One hundred and twenty men, women and children were fed to the Koban.

A cave had been found and was designated a holy place, an entrance to the underground realm where the gods lived and ate. The Koban were back doing what they are born to do: eat and build up a sustainable larder until time to mature and leave the planet for their own birthing journey into the stars.

Under their guidance and protection, the slow-witted Olmec flourish, their land now spread over a large area, many tribes now pay tribute in sacrifices to the gods. Many years pass, the Koban become fat and lazy.

Southern North America, 3000 Years Ago

Parvon Zin had been traveling across North America hunting down and killing the Koban as he found them; it was easy as a shapeshifter to gain trust of people when you can virtually be one of them. On a bright summer's day, in what would be known as Eagle Mountain in Arizona, Zin makes a grave mistake.

"THEY ARE STILL FOLLOWING US, SCALEMITE. I COUNTED TWENTY-THREE HEAT BLOOMS; IT MUST BE A WAR PARTY."

Zin scrambles up the mountain and makes his first mistake: it is a dead end! With a sheer drop to the rocky floor many feet below, he screams.

"TWO HELLS!"

"YOU HAVE THREE HUNDRED BEATS BEFORE THEY GET HERE, DO SOMETHING, SCALEMITE! REMEMBER TARRAG PEAK." (Zin's first flying lesson)

Long ago, Parvon Zin had shifted into a Pterosaur; to feel what it would be like to fly, he used this existing form and quickly shifted. Thirty beats later, just as the first couple of warriors came running around the rocky path, a seven-foot flying dinosaur soared over their heads. Zin spiralled up into the air on thermals rising from the valley and had a clear view of the entire area, he could see the Indian village. Steering well away from it, he landed on top a craggy hill. Shifting back to human Indian form, he spotted his second mistake, sitting cross-legged on a prayer mat was an old Indian shaman eyes wide, mouth open, staring at what could only be a 'Thunderbird' in human form, a changeling. Totally accepting what he had seen without reservation, the old shaman introduces himself to the thunderbird.

"I am Kodo, shaman of the Londa People. I have prayed for two days; my answer stands before me. Help us, mighty Thunderbird. Stop the raids of the Olmec slavers, my people have suffered for years; we keep moving north, but they still steal away my people." The old shaman slides to the ground unconscious.

"EAT HIM, HE IS OLD AND SCRAWNY, BUT HEY, MEAT'S MEAT."

"By the Great Serpent, Ohna."

"EAT A LEG THEN, HE HAS TWO."

"Ohna, please, I am starving, but I am not going to eat what might turn out to be a blessing."

"A HAND THEN, HE HAS TWO OF THEM AS WELL."

"OHNA! STOP!"

Bending down, Zin picks up the old man and starts down the slope towards the village, as he comes upon a shallow stream, the old man wakes up. Zin sets him down near the water, the old shaman and Zin drink their fill.

"Come, Thunderbird, you must be hungry. I know I am we will feast together."

With that, the two men walk into the village, shouts of joy rise up from the people as the old shaman shouts out that his prayers have been answered and for a feast to be laid out for the young god.

Zin is washed and given soft clothes and shoes to wear while the food is being prepared. Suckling pig…Zin loves these things and wolfs down three before you could say 'here little piggy'. He would rather have had them live but has gotten used to eating cooked food.

Zin is told a tale of woe so horrifying as to be unbelievable, but it soon becomes obvious he has found another clutch of Koban juveniles. Zin assures the tribe's people he will help stop the Olmec raiders.

His help comes later that same week, as three scouts come screaming into the village shouting warnings of Olmec warriors in the pass at the end of the valley. Zin, the old shaman and twelve warriors go to assess the situation. Lying in the long grass atop a small rise, they watch the Olmec arrogantly walk about below them; they already have several Indians roped together by the neck for transport back to their camp. There are twenty Olmec warriors.

Looking around at the small band of warriors, Zin speaks to the old shaman.

"Stay and watch, you will know when to go free the captives. I am more than a thunderbird."

Zin quickly strips to the amusement of the younger warriors and says to the old shaman, "As I said, I am more than a thunderbird."

With a slight sigh, his form shimmers, and thirty beats later, a seven-foot Velociraptor is squatting beside them, all twelve men fall backwards to get away from the fierce-looking beast, only the old shaman sits as he was, smiling. "Indeed."

"OOOOO, I LOVE YOU AS A VELOCIRAPTOR, YOU SEXY THING, YOU STAY LIKE THAT FOR A WHILE, LIFT YOUR TAIL, LET'S SEE Y-"

"TWO HELLS, OHNA, STOP PLEASE!"

"SPOILSPORT, I WOULD HAVE SHOWN YOU MINE."

"ENOUGH! I have enemies to worry about."

"GET SOME HEADS, BRAINS ARE GOOD FOR YOU, YOU ARE LOSING YOUR LUSTRE, YOUR SCALES ARE DULL, SIX HEADS SHOULD DO IT."

Shaking his head, he turns to the shaman and says, "Get the captives when I give the signal, meet back here, wait for me, and do not be afraid of what you see."

With that, he slinks towards the unsuspecting Olmec.

The outer guard was the first to go. Zin the Velociraptor hits him so hard he is decapitated by the strike to his neck; thinking of Ohna, he puts the head to the side for later.

"GOOD IDEA, SCALEMITE."

The next three are all sitting in a row slightly away from the captives, the outside two are hit simultaneously, two large scythe-like claws pierce their throats while the centre Olmec gets his face bitten off. All three die almost instantly.

"GET THE HEADS YOU DIM-WITTED DOGAL BEFORE SOMEONE STEALS THEM."

"QUIET, OHNA! I will get them later."

The rest of the Olmec are starting to herd the prisoners towards the rise where the Londa warriors and old shaman are.

By his fancy dress and headgear, the obvious leader of the Olmec gave himself away further by shouting orders and asking where the missing men were, time to move thought Zin.

With a loud hissing roar, Zin the Velociraptor tears into the group of Olmec, going straight for the leader, a leaping jump puts him on the man's back, the cruel claws tearing out great chunks of flesh, the man drops screaming to the ground, his men scatter in panic…Zin scythes repeatedly through the group of terrified warriors.

Zin has been forcing the Olmecs towards his small group. As they near the slight rise, Zin screams, "NOW! KILL THEM ALL!"

The twelve warriors slice into the frightened men. Obsidian knives and hatchets doing bloody work, within moments the little glade is still apart from low moans from the wounded, which are quickly silenced by driven blades.

The old shaman is over beside the petrified captives trying to assure them that they are not to be a feast of the terrible lizard. Meanwhile, the terrible lizard is on his sixth head. "Ohna's right, brains are just what I needed."

"TOLD YOU, SCALEMITE, YOU LOOK SHINIER ALREADY. OOOH, GO ON, LIFT YOUR TAIL, YOU KNOW YOU WANT TO. OOOOOO! NICE."

Back at the village, tales are being told of the great battle, the captives are welcomed into the tribe and Zin is now a hero GOD of great proportions; all is good.

All would have been just peachy if they had actually killed everyone!

The scale tick that got away told his story to PoNgbe/Turen of the Koban.

"Gather all my brothers and sister, we have a hunter to kill," growls Turen.

Luckily after the last group of Olmec had come through the pass, Zin had suggested that a permanent group of watchers be positioned on a ridge at the end of the valley; they spotted the massive Olmec army two days march away.

Word quickly reached Zin and the old shaman. Panic, pure raw panic went through the entire village. Zin tells the old shaman to calm the crowd. Zin takes a deep breath, strips out of his clothes and a shimmering thirty beats blur later squatted a Pterosaur.

Their thunderbird. Zin tells the old shaman he is off to see what the Olmec army is doing; with a great flap of leathery wings, he soars into the air to massed cheers from the villagers.

What Zin sees from above is a mass of campfire lights, thousands of men all camped waiting to enter the narrow steep-sided cut through the mountain, high walls one side and a two hundred feet fall on the other. Zin lands on an outcropping and studies the terrain…something is nagging at his subconscious.

"OOOOO THAT LOOKS JUST LIKE THERMOPYLAE, I MISS THE SPARTANS."

"OHNA! YOU ARE A GENIUS."

"I KNOW…EEEH! WHAT?"

"We become Spartans." Zin remembers back when he was nearly killed by the 'Kryptia'.

Sparta

Zin in the form of a Greek merchant was tracking a Koban clutch that was rumoured to be with the Persians helping them conquer virtually all of the Middle-East and about to attack the Greeks; it was unfortunate it was the start of August and Zin looked a lot like a local 'Helot'.

In August, the local Helots (meaning captives) are virtually fair game to be killed by any Spartan who comes across them, it was Zin's unlucky/lucky day.

Amendus was a 21-year-old Spartan warrior just one year out of his thirteen-year Agoge training programme, and full of vinegar and piss, he arrogantly shouts, "Hey you, Helot, stop!"

Zin does just that and turns to face the well-muscled arrogant young Spartan.

The Spartan is supremely confident of an easy kill of this 'subspecies' (as the Spartans thought of the Helots). He strides arrogantly up to the Helot/Zin, sliding out a dagger as he approaches.

Zin lets him get to arm's length then strikes, lightning quick! The palm of his hand hits and sticks to the Spartan's bare chest, fine tendrils enter the skin and enzymes flow, paralysing the Spartan.

Within thirty seconds, Zin is now in Spartan form with all memories and skills transferred.

Amendus/Zin stays with the Spartans for over a year, getting to genuinely like the austere but vibrantly loyal people; he hears from scouts along the border where the Koban are. Xerxes has powerful advisors helping him expand Persian rule, they are of course Koban; using a tried and tested technique, he bribes his way into the chosen few who will hold back the Persian onslaught.

He is to report to Leonidas as part of the three hundred who were to hold the 'Hot Gates' (Thermopylae), exactly where he needs to be to get access to the Koban.

Zin/Amendus walking along the road is soon joined by more and more Spartans as they march to their staging area just outside the Hot Gates. Leonidas greets them all.

"Brothers, we have been given a simple task, that is to hold the Hot Gates, this we will do." Lifting up his sword, he shouts, "SPARTA!"

So, three hundred men superbly trained, and using the natural funnel of the narrow pass, forged their names in history, holding back one hundred thousand Persian troops for three days, until a Greek called Ephialtes betrays them and shows the Persians a secret pass that allows them to get behind the Spartans.

None of the three hundred Spartans survive. Fighting to the last man.

Well, technically, Zin was not a man. Zin shifts into a Persian Elite Warrior and kills the small clutch of Koban who were helping Xerxes extend the Persian Empire.

Londa Village

Back in the village, a plan is drawn up. Zin recalls his Spartan training and puts it to good use.

'Shields', no one had even heard of shields, Zin had every warrior equipped with a newly made hoplon type shield.

Long spears were the next revelation, no one here used anything like this.

Finally, short stabbing daggers of sharpened hardened wood for using along with the shield.

All the warriors had their personal weapons of course but would train with the new weapons. Warriors all, they soon picked up the new tactics, each man protecting the man to his side with the shield, using the spears to hold and engage the enemy well away from the shield wall and short swords for close in work by the shield wall.

In one day, the warriors were semi-confident in their skills. There were not quite three hundred but two hundred and forty-three warriors were to hold the pass.

The narrowest part of the pass was fifty yards across. Eighty warriors standing side by side fill the space, two rows deep. Shields locked together, spears standing straight up, eight feet long. The two rows form the shield wall. With another two sets of eighty warriors to swap when the men at the front get weary, they had practised the tactics Zin had learned from the Spartans.

Water and food were brought up and medical shamans to treat any wounded.

They were ready; they did not have long to wait.

PoNgbe/Turen looks at the thin lines of only forty men each and laughed so loud he nearly wet himself. With a casual insulting wave of this arm, he sends in his leading wave of six hundred warriors into the pass to slaughter the enemy.

Supremely confident, they joke to each other bragging on how many heads they will take; they charged forward screaming 'OLMEC!'.

The six hundred men quickly started to get in each other's way as they are channelled into a constantly narrowing space. They were so tightly packed they could not raise their arms to bring weapons to bear. Most were at walking pace due to the congestion at the front.

When the Olmec are twenty feet away from the shield wall, the cry went up from Zin. "SPEARS!"

Eighty, eight feet long spears were brought down and held horizontal.

The Olmec virtually pushed themselves onto the spears. They had no option as they were being pushed from behind by comrades who could not see what was happening up front. The screams start and don't stop.

It is a slaughter! The front rows of Olmec who can see what's happening are desperately trying to go backwards.

The spears, smooth tips of hardened wood, are plunged in and out of bodies constantly, hundreds of dead and wounded are piling up in front of the shield wall.

"CHANGE!" screams Zin.

A quick practised shuffle of men and eighty fresh warriors appear in the front rows and continue the slaughter with fresh muscles. The weary warriors that had been at the front walk calmly back and rest taking drinks of water and bragging to each other about how many slavers they had killed.

The one-sided slaughter continues, this goes on for three changes before the Koban leader realises something is wrong and calls for a withdrawal.

SILENCE! All bar the moans of the wounded. The Olmec retreat back to the mouth of the pass and take stock only one hundred and twelve men return.

The Londa natives start working.

They gather the dead and build a wall across the gap, four bodies high.

This is used as a step, then a higher wall of eight bodies is formed, spears and captured swords protrude from the bodies forming a spiky barrier; some of the wall 'bricks' moan in pain, the Londa warriors leave them to it.

The Olmec bring forward bowmen, hundreds of them, with poison-tipped arrows; the sky darkens with arrows in flight from the Olmec, but again, the shields held up above the head is used as overhead cover and the body wall protects the defenders while the Londa bowmen can fire safely from behind this protection; it is again a one-sided slaughter.

No Londa warriors have yet been injured or killed.

The Koban are furious they have lost almost a third of their men. Scare tactics might work.

PoNgbe/Turen himself would shift into a 'God' and frighten the superstitious natives.

So going forward alone, PoNgbe/Turen in the form of a Draconian strides arrogantly up too but just out of arrow shot of the wall.

"HEAR ME, SURRENDER AND YOU WILL LIVE. RESIST US AND YOU WILL BE SENT TO THE UNDERWORLD TO DIE SCREAMING FOR ETERNITY." PoNgbe/Turen calls out from the Draconians form.

He is still in mid rant when Zin in Velociraptor form bounds over the wall, two clawed feet hit the Koban in the centre of its chest, throwing him to the ground, a single bite at the neck severs the head which is held up in one claw and thrown into the now screaming panicked Olmec front ranks. Standing tall, Zin screams out to the Olmec, "YOUR GODS ARE FALSE! THEY BETRAY YOU WITH LIES, SEND ME THE HEADS OF ALL OF YOUR FALSE GODS IN ORDER TO LIVE. DO IT NOW OR I WILL DEVOUR YOU ALL."

Within three hundred beats, twelve heads are lying in front of the shield wall and the Olmec are running back to their own lands, never once looking back.

Present Day

"WE NEED TO SHOW THE AMERICAN PEOPLE THAT THEY ARE FALSE GODS, THE SAME AS WE DID WITH THE OLMEC. FIGURATIVELY SPEAKING, SCALEMITE."

"That's the idea, Ohna, we have lived with these people for so long now I don't know if I would go home after we deal with the Koban."

The information gleaned from the human lieutenant who must have been fairly high up in the organisation was vast. They found out that only fifty-eight Koban were still alive worldwide. Sixteen had been killed in the Dulce Base Battle. Twenty-eight were left in the US.

Six were in Russia and the final eight were in China. Typical Koban selecting living areas within the most powerful nations on 'Earth'.

What a name for a planet! 'Dirtball' he had jokingly called it so long ago, then to find out they actually named it Earth was too much, one of the constantly amusing things Zin found with Earthlings. Dirtlings. Soilpeople! The jokes could be endless. Zin preferred 'Terans', it at least sounded okay.

"Ohna, we will set the seed of that here, first by using David Ike's protégée Tom Marks. We give Marks some evidence, show him some film from Dulce Base and let him do his thing."

Tom Marks was in hiding in a remote cabin totally off the grid, no phones or anything traceable; he was writing up his next exposé on how the country was being run by a shadow government ruled by reptilians who came from Middle Earth through great openings in the icecaps. The knock at his cabin door made him jump. It was followed with the cry of 'FEDEX!'.

A frightened Tom Marks accepts the bulky package from the FedEx driver and retreats into the cabin, looking around in all directions before shutting the door. Who the hell knew where he was staying? He was starting to panic even worse when a mobile phone slid out of the large padded envelope. He literally shits himself when the phone rang with the theme to *The X-Files*. Who says shapeshifters have no sense of humour?

"Mr Marks, listen carefully." Marks gets the full story, everything!

It is the equivalent of lighting the blue touch paper on a firecracker and stepping back…BOOOOOOM. Marks is now a weapon of mass distribution; he will investigate the living hell out of this.

Knowing the US side is underway with Tom Marks, John Running Fox/Zin and his acid tongued AI heads for Moscow.

Moscow (Savelovsky Market)

Victor Ivanovich Zukin/Telessi of the Koban had risen to Alpha male status in 1908 when the alpha female Galenn exploded inside her pod three miles above the Tunguska forest in Russia.

She had been trying out a new method of gaining escape velocity (Stolen from Nicholas Tesla) when it failed dramatically.

The force of the explosion levelled an eight hundred and thirty square mile radius of forest with a blast a thousand times more powerful than the soon-to-be discovered and used Hiroshima bomb.

Victor Ivanovich Zukin/Telessi did not usually get his hands dirty with Bratva (Brotherhood) business but this, THIS required a very strong response that only he could deliver.

Zukin in human form was typically Russian featured, looking a bit like Yuri Gagarin the soviet astronaut.

In the early days of the old USSR, this piece of shit would have gone to the Gulag, where the Koban had their human feed stock held prior to processing as food, but now, he would go to the pigs.

Zukin/Telessi was in a backroom of a butcher's shop sitting comfortably in a plush office chair. "So, Sergey Leonovich Tsepov, what have you to say about my missing shipment?"

The badly beaten, naked man was suspended between two burly enforcers slowly shaking his head back and forth, blood from a broken nose splashing to both sides.

"Nothing? That's a shame." Zukin/Telessi nods his head towards an industrial mincing machine.

The two enforcers drag the now screaming man over to the machine, they lift him over the edge of the hopper, feeding him in, feet first.

Tough man, he screamed all the way down to his waist.

"Collect five kilos of the mince, I will take it back to the Dacha," says Zukin/Telessi with a wave of his arm. Zukin/Telessi lived in the 'Rublevka' area, bordering the Podushkinskoe Forest. Very elite, secluded and secure. Back in his Dacha, he calls a meeting of his Koban brothers.

Sitting around a table in Draconian form, using their proper names not their human cover names, they gobble down freshly minced human flesh.

"Delicious, Telessi, we should do this more often." With a lift of a glass of ice-cold Vodka Massic, his second in command salutes him. The others at the table, Kree, Potlax, Yingsu and Amina join in the toast…KOBAN!

KNOCK! KNOCK!

"Enter," cries Telessi.

In walks a blinded servant, all of Telessi's servants are blind, either from birth or by removal of the eyes on becoming a servant; all can find their way through the building without aid.

"A phone call for you, Master Telessi." Holding out a mobile phone, the servant/slave hands it to his master.

"WHAT? Wait, say that again…The entire shipment? EVERYTHING? ALL OF IT! GGGRRRAAAAGGGGG!"

Looking around at his hatchmates he says, "I may have minced the wrong human. Another shipment of food stock has gone missing."

John Running Fox/Zin and his strike group of men from the Dulce raiders and the Apaches open the cargo container and release the one hundred and twenty small children aged between three and five years old, packed in like sardines.

The kids had been due to be the Koban's food stock.

"Call the *Politsiya* (police), tell them to come get the hatchlings!" John shouts over to Duke.

"NO ONE'S LOOKING, SCALEMITE, EAT THE SMALL ONE WITH THE RED HAIR. SEE IF IT TASTES LIKE DURGO."

"TWO HELLS, OHNA, I WILL NOT EAT A HUMAN HATCHLING! They do look delicious though. Hehehehe."

"LICK ONE AT LEAST FOR ME."

Bending down next to the little redhead who was sucking her thumb, John gives the top of her head a kiss and says in flawless Russian, "You will be okay, little one." To Ohna, he whispers, "Durgo, just like Durgo."

"THOUGHT SO." Giggles upon giggles follow.

Turning to face his men, he raises one hand holding up two fingers. "The two shipments we have stopped should get us a reaction, let's see what serpent wriggles out of the woodpile. Get to your sources and ask questions, you have plenty of Rubles to grease any tongues; if you need to get heavy, give me a call, now go! Get to Golyyanovo, Lublino and especially Savelovsky Market and start rattling cages," says John/Zin with a devilish grin.

Zukin/Telessi's Dacha, Rublevka

"People are asking questions in Savelovsky Market, boss. Golyanovo and Lublino districts as well. Our man in the *Politsiya* says the shipment of kids has been taken into protective custody and sent to a local children's home; we don't know which one," reports Aniton Blodesky, a mid-level enforcer with the Bratva.

"Find out who is asking questions, lean on the people, let them know that I love mince."

Savelovsky Market Moscow

"I have a lead, John, we found a group of local hard men beating up a couple of guys who had given us some good intel. You want to have a word with them, we have them at the warehouse you rented in the market," says Donald Firemaker on the phone.

"Yes, Donald, I will be there soon, tie them naked onto chairs, show them that big bowie knife you have; I will be with you soon." Folding the phone shut, John/Zin drives over to the warehouse.

Greeting Donald Firemaker and the seven men he brought over, he introduces himself to the naked tied-up men all sitting facing him in a neat row in fluent Russian.

"*Privet, Ty govoris Po Englessi?*" (Hello, do you speak English?)

Three shake their heads, one nods and says, "*Da.*"

With a nod from John, three of his men using razor sharp machetes decapitate the non-English-speaking Russians. Blood sprays everywhere, the fourth man screams out in horror as one of the heads lands in his lap.

"Good, we need you to take a message to your boss." Leaning down right into the man's face, John hisses, "*TY POIMAYESH?*" (Do you understand?)

"*D-D-DAA, D-Daaaa,*" stammers the man.

"Here's the message: We are here for your leaders, all six of them. Give them to us and we go home. You can then take over the Bratva. We don't care who runs the show, we won't interfere, and we only want the top six. *TY PONIMAYESH!*" (Do you understand?)

"*DA!*"

"Cut him loose. Give him the heads as a going away present." John folds his arms and watches as the man dresses and runs out the door, three heads swinging in a grocery bag leaving a trail of blood droplets.

It takes four more hits on local Bratva OPG (organised crime) businesses and fifteen heads before they get a result.

John gets a phone call; he had given every messenger the number of a burner phone…It starts ringing. A heavy Russian accent says, "We need to talk."

Sergei Gregorovich Mikhailov

He is tall at 6 ft 6. With a lean long face, a scar running from his right eyebrow to the tip of his right ear gives him an evil look.

With the scar, he looks exactly like your stereotypical German SS Officer. The short cropped blonde hair finishing off the effect.

He is the leader of the '*Soinjevskaya*' Bratva. And rival to the Koban-run '*Moskva*' Bratva.

Mikhailov sits by the window of an upmarket Moscow coffee shop, his bodyguards scattered through the shop and outside keeping watch, waiting patiently on the person who answered the burner phone.

"*Privet! Tovarich* Mikhailov, let's talk business." John slips into the booth across from the Bratva gang boss.

"HOW DID YOU GET PAST MY SECURITY?" Mikhailov looks desperately around for his security people.

"They're busy, don't worry they will not be harmed, I just want to talk. Coffee?"

So over coffee, John lays out the plan that will put Sergei Gregorovich Mikhailov in complete control of all the Bratva clans in the Moscow area, if not all of Russia.

"Your hatred of these men must be great, but Da, we will help. I have had someone inside their organisation for years, he will get us in, and you will have your heads. I have always admired Zukin's Dacha in Rublevka, after this it will be mine. I will contact you within one week. *DoSvidanja, Tovarich* (goodbye, friend)." Mikhailov stands, nods and walks calmly out of the coffee shop.

Three days later, six beautifully polished wooden boxes, the size of hat boxes, are delivered to the warehouse in Savelovsky Market containing six neatly decapitated heads. The Russian clutch of Koban is no more.

"ARE THEY STILL FRESH? EAT THEM, EAT THEM, OOOOOOH, LOOK AT THAT, THE TOP CAME OFF NEAT JUST LIKE AN EGG, NICE. DID YOU KNOW YOUR SLURP IS VERY LOUD, SCALEMITE?"

As a parting gift, Sergei Mikhailov sends word of an ongoing trade deal the Russian Koban had with the Chinese Tong Gangs regarding opium shipments in payment for live human cargo.

John has a lead towards his next target. A warehouse on Hainan Dao Island, run by the Chinese Koban.

Hainan Dao Island, China

"Vivan, this is Telessi. I have just learned we have a hunter after us. He has left many messages stating he will kill all of us. We know it's a hunter because he called us Koban, no human knows that name. We are taking all precautions. Be sure you do the same."

"I will, old friend, I will. Take care, tell me when you are eating this scale buffer's intestines."

Forewarned, Vivan gathers her seven Koban hatchmates and plans for the utter destruction of this scale-torn hunter. Unaware that later that same day Telessi and his hatchmates lost their heads.

Seated around a large ornate black lacquered wooden table dating back to the Han Dynasty, Vivan stands and looks at her seven surviving hatchmates, three female and four male Koban, a rare batch indeed with four males and four females left in the clutch. The males are all tall and lithe with sculpted muscles and smooth handsome oriental faces, looking not unlike Bruce Lee. All are Shaolin trained martial art experts, trained hundreds of years ago in the Shaolin Quan Temple in Henan Province.

The female Koban were beautiful Chinese women with delicate features, slim well-formed bodies, very similar in looks to Lucy Liu and like their brother's experts in martial arts, though more towards the Japanese Ninja style, all had trained in Japan in an exclusive all women Ninja Temple producing silent deadly assassins.

John many years ago had actually met one of the Koban in China, an army lieutenant named Cho, but at the time, it was an 'enemy of my enemy is my friend' kind of thing.

China, 1942

Sergeant Harry Arbuckle, sometimes known as ParVon Zin, was in China under the guise of an American Sergeant with 'Y Force', training Chinese troops to fight the Japanese.

This endeavour was solely to gain him access to China where he had heard a clutch of eight Koban were entrenched.

With WW2 in full swing, getting around the world was downright dangerous to say the least, how he got this far was a story in itself.

He had received a message from an Australian coast watcher of a sighting of an unbelievable spectacle that no one but Harry Arbuckle/Zin and his (as worldwide as he could get) group of watchers would believe. A large reptile-like creature had totally wiped out a Japanese coastal defence gun unit, then fled in a Chinese junk, heading towards Chinese waters.

More local talk of a cursed island full of dragons, mysterious disappearances, man-eating reptiles drew Zin's attention to China and the only way he could get there was with the US military.

How in the two hells was he going to do that!

Fort Lewis 1941

Harry Arbuckle was a brutish, bully of a man. Six feet and seven inches tall, fairly handsome but with mean-looking features because of the permanent sneer he adopted.

Always throwing his weight about and being very, very heavy handed with the local hookers, one rumour said he had killed a whore at his last base, but no proof was found. He was now stationed in Fort Lewis near Washington.

ParVon Zin's extensive list of informants included local hookers; these women gleaned a lot of information from their clients. Zin paid well for it.

Rose Taylor was a hooker who ran afoul of Arbuckle, he beat her so badly she nearly died. In desperation, her friends called Zin and told the story. Zin had been looking for a way to China. Arbuckle would be that vessel.

Arbuckle was drunk, as usual, and he was a mean drunk.

He kicked open the door to the 'White Lilly Whore House' near the base, the doorman gave him a look, but he was afraid of the big army sergeant so never did anything, even though he knew he beat up the girls.

Arbuckle arrogantly strode in and shouted to the madam, "Send out your whores, you old bitch!"

Looking fearful, all the girls come out, dressed in their usual lack of clothes.

Arbuckle leers at them all, an almost fully recovered Rose calls over.

"Sergeant, we don't want any trouble, please let ALL of us give you a night you won't believe." This was delivered in silky, sultry tones.

Arbuckle gasps. "All of you whores want me?"

"Yes, stud, we ALL want you real bad," breathe the girls seductively.

"Come to daddy then, I got what you want," he says grabbing and shaking his crotch. He is panting with lust.

"Come on then, stud, in here." With seductive winks, the girls walk into the room. As Arbuckle walks through the door, Zin's punch knocks him flat on his back, unconscious before he hits the floor.

Arbuckle wakes up naked and strapped to a sturdy chair.

"Okay, ladies, he is all yours. All I ask is that you do not kill him. I can use his body in any shape as long as he is alive. You okay with that?" Zin nods and pats Arbuckle's cheek saying, "Enjoy, stud."

Eight stone-faced, abused whores slowly walk around the bound man. Zin watches from the far corner.

The screams start just a moment later.

"OOOOOO! I HAVE NOT SEEN THAT IN AGES. REMEMBER THAT APACHE WOMAN WHO GOT HOLD OF THE CAVALRY MAN, SHE DID THE SAME THING. ASK FOR THEM WHILE THEY'RE HOT! SEE WHAT THEY TASTES LIKE."

"TWO HELLS, OHNA, I AM NOT EATING A MAN'S BALLS."

"I BET THEY TASTE LIKE DURGO, OOOOO, LOOK! ASK HIM WHAT THEY TASTE LIKE, ASK HIM, SCALEMITE, ASK HIM."

"TWO HELLS, OHNA, HOW CAN HE ANSWER WITH HIS MOUTH FULL?" The memory triggered by the torture sends Zin back to another similar scene over a hundred years before.

Apache Camp, the Day After the Cieneguilla Victory, 1854

Liluye (hawk singing), a beautiful Apache woman, wiped the bowie knife clean and looked down without compassion at what was left of trooper Silas Parkins.

The year 1854, the 1st Cavalry had been pursuing a fleeing Apache war band, but unknown to them, a force of two hundred and twenty Jicarilla Apache waited in ambush. The sixty-trooper force is taken completely by surprise, within minutes twenty-two are dead and thirty-six are wounded, the battle drags on for four hours, then the Apache leave victorious.

Trooper Silas Parkins had heard enough stories, seen enough evidence of why you did not let yourself be captured by the Apache.

He knew he was doomed, being wounded and without a horse he had no hope, so with one bullet left he stuck the Colt single action .45 in his mouth and without hesitation pulled the trigger…CLICK! Misfire or miscount, Silas was fucked.

The Apache surround the trooper and let their horses stamp him into unconsciousness.

Zin in the form of a Hopi Indian shaman had been in the village gathering information about evil Kachina spirits (Koban) when he sees poor Silas's end.

The balls always seem to be the first to go. Dispassionately, Zin watches as the Apache squaws virtually dismantle trooper Parkins chunk by bloody chunk.

White Lilly Whore House

The women work on Arbuckle for almost three hours before Zin finally steps in and stops it.

"Remember, ladies, you will see this pile of poop again, but he will be a completely different person."

Rose has explained to the others what Zin can do, they all nod in agreement and leave the room to wash the blood off, some of them have splatters right up past their elbows.

Thirty beats later and Zin stands as a fully shapeshifted, reassembled with re-attached plumbing, fingers, toes, nose, ears, nipples Sergeant Harry Arbuckle.

He dresses in Arbuckle's uniform and walks out the door. Outside, he walks up to the hookers and gives them all a tender hug and kiss, giving Rose a small pile of cash, which was every cent Arbuckle had on him.

"Thanks, Rose, goodbye, girls." Arbuckle/Zin walks out the door. The tearful, thankful whores wave goodbye.

The doorman shakes his head at this scene. "Women can't understand them one bit."

Training Camp, Southern Mainland China

Sergeant Harry Arbuckle/Zin had been in China for two months and genuinely liked the Chinese people and was starting to get a real hate for the Japanese though, after hearing first-hand tales of massacres and the torture of Chinese civilians and soldiers. Lately, he had been hearing of a squad of Chinese soldiers that were tearing through Japanese troops like paper, the Japanese soldiers called them 'Akuryo Heishi' (Demon Soldiers). Bodies of the dead Japanese were never found. He finally came across the unit that had been stalking the Japanese as he was leaving China. Before leaving to return to the States to train American soldiers, he was to be given a medal from Chiang Kai-Shek himself, for his outstanding assistance to the Chinese military, as he was being given his medal.

"KOBAN! KOBAN! THERE ARE KOBAN NEAR."
"Where, Ohna? WHERE!"
"THIRTY FEET TO YOUR LEFT."
Looking left, Arbuckle/Zin spots a Chinese officer waiting in line to receive his medal for fighting the Japanese. Their eyes lock.

"Step forward, Lieutenant Cho." The Koban/Cho walks forward and receives his medal, one for supreme service to his country; as he salutes and moves back into line, Arbuckle/Zin is waiting.

"I know what you are. What you have done! What you will do if you leave this planet. At this moment in time, 'the enemy of my enemy is my friend.' So be it. We will meet again, and when we do, one of us will die, you have my word on that." Arbuckle/Zin steps back.

The Koban bows from the waist and says in broken English, "An honourable foe is always welcome. Hear this, Sergeant, you will have an honourable battle from us, I look forward to taking your head as a trophy and placing it in our war room, but I give you fair warning, my sisters will not give you a fair fight, so be aware. The female of our species is far more deadly than the male." With a final bow, Lieutenant Cho walks over to the waiting Chinese officers.

Arbuckle/Zin heads to an army deuce and a half truck and is driven to an airstrip where a C47 transport plane starts his long journey back to the States.

Ju Dian Hainan Dao Island, Present Day

Vivan stands before her hatchmates. "What do we know of this hunter, other than he is in Russia."

Cho stands and addresses the room.

"We know, or assume, that there is only one hunter. As you know, I met him here in China during the war; he was an honourable man. He will of course have changed his appearance since then, we need photographs from our Russian brothers. His honour may be his weakness; it is my belief that our sisters may be our best weapon in defeating this killer and should take the lead, with us (sweeping his arm towards the seated males) backing up your play."

"It will be so." She nods towards her three sisters. "Come, sisters, we have mischief to plan." Vivan leads the way out of the room.

The four Koban females, Vivan, Dena, Fonda and Onina retreat down into the bowels of the massive castle-like house called Ju Dian (Stronghold) into their private rooms where they have tortured and played with many a male and female victim over the hundreds of years that they have lived on the island.

The locals have horror stories from long past of the evil Akuryo (demons) that live on the island. Nothing could be more different than the legends that are associated with Ju Dian castle though. The four brothers Cho, Chan, Sulu and Vinux are renowned through the years for honourably defending the island and its people from invaders. The clash of interests was sometimes cause for argument between the siblings. Promises of captive enemy warriors for the females to deal with and local criminals usually kept the more aggressive females in check and gave them something to play with; screams from underground were not an uncommon sound in the castle. The locals always gave the place a very, very wide berth.

Basuo Port, Donfang City, Hainan Dao

John Running Fox/Zin and his squad of twenty-five, now seasoned fighters, arrive on port on a chartered fishing boat. To keep to the expected tourist routine and try to glean some information, they head for the nearest club. This is on Youyi North Road and it's a place called The Basuogang Workers Club.

John, Donald and six men grab a minibus taxi and get dropped at the club; they wander in and order a round of beers; settling down around a table, they absorb the atmosphere and keep their ears open for information.

John is the only one who speaks Chinese but does not let on, locals are usually more likely to talk between themselves especially if the stupid western tourists don't know you are talking about them.

"What are they saying? Come on, Chang, you speak the language," one small guy at the bar asks the barkeeper.

"You are too nosy, Huan. They are talking about fishing and may be going inland hunting," grunts Chang while cleaning a beer glass.

"We should send them up to Ju Dian and let the evil spirits play with them," the smaller man jokes.

In perfect Mandarin, John/Zin says, "And what spirits would that be?"

Spraying out a mouthful of beer, the small man splutters out, "Sorry, good sir, I meant no offence." Quickly standing up from his barstool, he barely comes level with John's chest.

John looks down and says, "Let me buy you a drink, we are very interested in hearing about spirits; come join us, we will supply the booze for a good story."

Two hours later and a very drunk local has told them all about the stories surrounding Ju Dian castle.

Next day on the boat, a battle plan is worked out.

"We need information, John, this place is a virtual fortress by what Huan said. Send Jack and Willie up to scope it out. They are our scout sniper team, nearly as good as us Apache (Laughs from the pair follow). Let them go up and fix up a hide and do some snooping, take the Barret and back up weapons, one of the radios. We then go on their information," Donald Firemaker says.

The other men are not involved at this point as the snipers usually worked on their own.

"Sounds good, do it," says John walking away.

John/Zin turns and walks into the interior cabin and addresses the sixteen others who are seated in the cabin on benches and chairs, pointing at the map on the table with the tip of a pencil (only amateurs use their fingers) and says, "Smithy, you pick five guys and go up to the lake below the fortress, set up camp and pretend you are fishing. Wait until Jack and Willie are set up. Donald, you and the Apache are with me, with our skin colour we blend in better than the D-Naa white eyes."

This brought on guffaws of laughter from the remaining men on the boat.

John turns towards the last group of ten men and says.

"You guys are our backup, keep the radio manned at all times; we all good?" Nods in return from all the guys.

"Okay! Let's do this."

Jack and Willie steal a car from a rundown area near the dock, the beat-up Nissan looked terrible but ran well. Using a handheld GPS unit, they head for the hills. A two-hour drive finds them in a secluded area above the lake. They give the old Nissan its first and last swimming lesson, it does not do well and sinks to the bottom of the lake after running down a steep embankment and plunging into the water. Sinking totally out of sight. Packed up like Sherpas, the two-man sniper team head up towards the castle. After a four-hour trek, they find the perfect place and start making up their sniper's perch. It is a cleft in the rocky hill overlooking the castle one mile away. It has natural bushes growing around it so it's only a matter of clearing out a space in its centre and setting up home; they have an in and out doorway, front and rear of the cleft. Going down their back trail, they set up a claymore mine and an infra-red warning 'trip wire'. To their blind sides, two more claymores are set up; feeling quite secure they settle in and begin their reconnaissance.

"Spartan six, this is Spartan three radio check, we are set and in position, radio checks every thirty, over," Willie whispers into the radio.

"Spartan three. Spartan six receiving loud and clear, checks every thirty minutes confirmed." Continuing he addresses the last ten men who would stay on the boat.

"Mike, you and the rest stay on the boat, monitor the radio, you are Spartan one, you have the backup radio set, so with both of us monitoring Spartan three, we should not miss anything. You are also the cavalry."

The ten men on the boat start shouting good-natured jabs at the eight Apache Indians saying the cavalry would come save their red asses. John and the seven Apache give as good as they get, all leave in good humour.

John had not told any of the others his plans, because at this point he did not have any and would not until something broke loose, so his little group headed up into the mountains in a rented van to do some mountaineering, as good a cover as any, this would put him in the area if anything happened.

"Simpson!" One of Andy Smith's men turn around, a lank-haired weasel of a man.

"No more fucking about with the local women, plenty of time for that later."

Simpson was a sleazy asshole who could not keep it in his pants; the other men were starting to complain about his attitude; after this, he would tell John to cut him loose as soon as they hit US soil.

It happened on day two, as Simpson and his sidekick, Oscar Pindan, drove to the nearest town for supplies. They had loaded up the van with fresh food and a crate of local beer; they were half a mile out from town on their way back when Simpson squealed.

"PUSSY!"

Walking along the road were two stunning Chinese women in their mid-twenties; they looked close enough alike to be sisters, to Simpson they all looked the same anyway. He crawls by in the van with the window open leering openly at the women, he calls out suggestively, "Want a ride?"

The women give each other a look that is missed by the ogling Simpson and now openly leering Oscar Pindan. Their informant in the grocery store had been spot on, Dulan would be rewarded.

With a small bow, the women smile and say, "Thank you."

"Great, you speak American, we don't know any Chink talk, come on, ladies, climb in," says a leering Simpson.

There is a bench seat behind the drivers, the two women climb in and settle down.

Simpson turns and starts to talk to the women, when both of them draw out tasers and zap both men unconscious.

Pindan surfaces first, he is naked and staked out on the grass, arms and legs spread painfully apart; he is lying next to the van which is now off the road and in a small clearing beside some trees.

Getting right to business, Vivan and her second in command Onina start getting information, their way.

"Secateurs please, dear sister!" Pindan screams as his testicles drops from his body. This wakes up a similarly staked naked Simpson.

The two Koban siblings systematically chop Pindan into bite-sized morsels, which they eat in front of a terrified screaming Simpson. Not a question has been asked, the sisters engage in small talk amongst themselves as they feast on Pidan.

"Could you please cut me a slice of that rather nice-looking kidney?" Pindan had stopped screaming quite a while ago, around about when Onina asked for a portion of liver. Simpson was now just whimpering. Licking her fingers clean, Vivan looks down on Simpson and pleasantly says, "Hello, and what is your name."

Simpson tells them everything, absolutely everything. The sisters take the van up to Ju Dian. Simpson untouched and quietly weeping is lying in the cargo bay.

Spartan three calls in, "Blue van driven into the castle by two Chinese women, Spartan three out."

Back at the fishing camp, the four other men, Andy Smith, Enrique Gonzales, Greg Young and David Wilson are wondering where Simpson and Pindan have gone.

"We should never have sent those two assholes into town, they are probably chasing skirt," Smithy moans.

With the information gleaned by the sisters from Simpson, the four brothers go after the forward 'fishing' base.

"Do you want prisoners, sister?" Cho calls over his shoulder as he walks out.

"Of course, we haven't had any playthings for such a long time, so alive and well if you please, brother," says Vivan with a sweet smile.

The fishing camp is taken within seconds of the brother's arrival. It was childishly easy for the exquisitely trained Koban.

Four unconscious men are delivered to an ecstatic bunch of women who are jumping up and down like teenagers clapping their hands together after being given new toys, which is exactly what they have been given.

"Fresh meat tonight, brothers, what cuts would you all prefer, we can do whatever you like."

"Could you find out if one of them is the leader please? If possible, I would like to fight him in honourable combat."

"Certainly, my brother, he shall be all yours, his head will be preserved and placed in the trophy room with all the rest you have vanquished. Can you send Dulan ten thousand Yuan for the information that got us the strangers?" With a slight bow and swish of skirts, she heads down to the playroom.

The five survivors find themselves tied to X frames totally naked, legs and arms spread wide. The X frames formed a circle around the walls of the circular chamber, the prisoners could see each other, four were stoically silent, Simpson was continuously whimpering, he had pissed and shit himself already.

The Koban females came in and tut-tutted about the smell and mess. Fonda the fourth sister draws down a hose from its reel and sprayed Simpson until he was clean, then washed the mess down a drain in the middle of the room, the white floor to ceiling tiles made this so easy.

"Gentlemen, I am going to ask you all to tell me where your leader is, we know his name is John Running Fox, which we all think is so cute, but where is this delightfully named man? Let me introduce you to my sisters." In walks three Koban in their Draconian reptilian form of upright-walking dinosaurs, still noticeably female in form, but the teeth and claws were a definite turn off.

"This is Dina." Dina does a perfect little curtsey.

"This is Fonda." Fonds gives a sharp bow.

"This is Onina." Onina licks her lips.

"And I am VIVAN…GGGGRRRRAAWWWWLLLLLLL!" The female Koban hunting challenge cry bounces off the walls. Now stripped naked, she changes before the terrified screaming men. Simpson has already passed out with fear. The other four men get the individual attention of one of the Koban. It is just as well the place is easily cleaned.

Simpson awakens to silence, except for a constant dripping, which he finds to his horror is blood dripping from the eviscerated corpses of the men around him. Obvious chunks of flesh have been removed as per the instructions for dinner; he finds himself free from the X frame and cleaned up sitting against a clean section of the room. Puzzled, he stands just at that point the door opens and in walk the four Koban males who asked for their meal to be served fresh, live and kicking; they tear him apart eating from each limb first before equally quartering the torso…delicious.

"Spartan three calling in, it's nineteen thirty hours Local time, there may be a party going on, we can see shadows moving but nothing distinct, Spartan three out."

"Received, Spartan three." Donald Firemaker changes channels.

"Come in, Spartan two. Come in, Spartan two?" …Nothing.

"John, Spartan two is not responsive," a worried Donald Firemaker says.

"Call Spartan three. Say we might have lost Spartan two, tell them to sit tight and report." John worriedly paces the campsite three miles to the west of Spartan two.

"I am going to check it out, I will be back soon, you are better not seeing this so get the guys into the tent come out in five minutes."

They come out to a pile of clothes and equipment, but no John.

John had stripped and shifted into the Pterosaur; with a whoosh of wings, he is way over the treetops. In just a couple of minutes, he is circling the campsite; it is obvious there was a struggle. John can't land and chance risking the thirty-beat window where he is totally defenceless so he gets as low as possible, no sign of any of the men; he can smell blood though. Back at the mountain campsite, he quickly redresses and briefs his men.

"It's still neat how you do that no matter how many times I see it, boss," says Duke Geneva with a big cheesy grin. John had shown his closest men what he could do and introduced Ohna. That was a hilarious day, the guys freaked out. John being John had shown them every *Jurassic Park* film first of course.

"Spartan one report." Donald Firemaker is still on the line when they hear.

"Spartan six we are—" Bang! Indistinct grunts, thuds, a piercing scream…Then static!

"FUCK! WHAT THE HELL JUST HAPPENED?" screams Firemaker. "Spartan one, Spartan one, come in, Spartan one." Firemaker's panicky voice comes over the speaker in the boat.

A cultured Chinese voice speaking in English says, "May I speak with your leader please, my name is Cho."

John/Zin's head swings around at hearing Cho's voice again after so many years. "Let me speak to him, Donald."

"What do you want, Cho?" questions John.

"Ahh, is that you, Sergeant Arbuckle? After all this time, how are you?"

"What did you do to my men, Cho?"

"They all died, clean honourable deaths, Sergeant, unlike your men at the lake, my sisters were given them. Not so clean or honourable, I am afraid."

"Bastard! I am coming for you, Koban, you will have your fight and I will put you in the ground."

With a cutting action across his throat from John, Firemaker cuts the radio connection to the boat.

"Get me Spartan three," growls John.

"SPARTAN THREE, FIRE MISSION, TAKE OUT ALL TARGETS OF OPPORTUNITY YOU SEE. KILL AS MANY AS YOU CAN THEN BUG OUT TO THESE CO-ORDINATES!" John screams down the handset.

"Spartan six, Spartan three. Copy," say the cool, calm voice of spotter Willie Hawkins.

"Well, Willie, get on that spotting scope and find me some targets," drawls Jake.

They had every window scoped in, front door, side door, balcony, every possible place was ranged, scoped and doped and listed on his sniper's data card. He was ready.

"Target! Front right window, distance one thousand four hundred and ninety yards. Wind from the right," whispers Willie.

"Got it, two mil dots across four up ready." This would be in sniper talk a 'cold shot', first shot fired through a cold barrel.

"Wind steady, take your shot," calm spotter's response.

Letting out a slow breath, fingertip just touching the trigger, a gentle squeeze and POW!

The suppressed Barret was still loud (only movie silencers were silent) but not loud enough to be heard near on a mile away.

Just under two seconds later and the large 50 cal. bullet takes Fonda's head completely off her body. No one in the castle hears a thing.

Snick, snick. Jake works the smooth as silk bolt, another match grade 50 cal. bullet slides into the breach.

"Target down! Clean kill," whispers Willie.

"New target! Front door, one thousand five hundred and thirty-nine yards, target stationary, wind now zero," says his spotter.

Going off a hot barrel now, his sniper calculations are easier to make.

"Got it," breathes Jake.

Through the scope, the target is sitting by the front door with a cup of something, tea? Reading a paper.

"On target two mil dots up zero across."

"Take your shot," whispers Willie.

POW! Snick, snick as the bolt is worked and the brass casing spirals to the side catching the light.

The round hit right between the eyes. Cranial vault shot, instant death. The wall behind the Koban Dina has a large red sunburst pattern on it.

"No target, no targ…wait! Partial target at the side door, wait! Wait! Moving target walking to the barn." Willie's voice is icy calm.

The barn was their furthest scoped point at dead on a mile, one thousand seven hundred and sixty yards, which in sniping distances was still point blank.

"Target moving to the barn." Calm spotter's voice.

Jake squirmed to his right a little following the woman with the Leupold scope.

"On target, on target," whispers Jake.

"Take your shot when she opens the door," advises Willie.

"On target, same setting two mills up zero across, on target," Jake breathes out.

POW! Snick, snick, new round chambered.

Onina's head explodes from the rear to front blowing her face off. The door is splashed crimson.

"Searching? No target, no target." Willie rubs his eyes with his GO rag.

Vivan is sitting in her office blissfully unaware she is now the sole surviving Koban female in China.

"Spartan three, Spartan six. Abort! Abort! Abort! Bug out, meet us at rally point seven."

It's Vivan's lucky day. She does not find out what has happened to her hatchmates until Cho bursts in with the news one hour later.

"Search the area, find out who did this!" screams Vivan.

They spread out and search, combing the area looking for what they now know is a sniper's nest somewhere.

Two of the brothers Chan and Sulu coming in from different sides both investigating a low electronic hum coming from a cleft in the hill, they signal each other to move in. A radio had been left as a lure broadcasting static; it worked a treat.

CRACK, BOOOM, CRACK BOOOOM. The noise echoing from the hills.

The two brothers hit the trip wires almost at the same time. Seven hundred, one eighth inch ball bearings from the Claymore mines disintegrates the two Koban into a fine red mist.

"How many did we get?" asks John as he conducts a mini debrief.

"We definitely got three of the females, clean kills. And the two explosions we heard possible pair wounded or dead we don't know for sure," Willie said.

"Let's ask the bastard." Switching on the phone, John calms his voice and says, "How's the family, Cho?"

"You do not fight with honour but strike from hiding and place traps. I WILL RIP OUT YOUR SPINE WHILE YOU LIVE!" screams Cho.

"That's not very nice, I asked a civil question. Hurts doesn't it? Listen, you Koban bastard, I am coming for you to finish this, see you real soon." John switches off the phone with a grim smile.

John turns to Donald and says, "Who turned us over to the Koban, we need to find them. We need to get them someplace where we can ambush them, feed them false information, set up a kill zone."

"Boss, some asshole in the grocery store the guys got supplies from is throwing money about like no one's business, back when I was an enforcer with big Franky that usually meant a squealer had just been paid."

"Go lean on him, Duke, if it pans out, bring him here," John hisses.

Two hours later, Duke drags in a sobbing, skinny Chinese man, wet piss stains down the front of his powder blue pants' leg.

"This is Dulan and he is sorry as hell he let the Koban bitches have our guys." Duke's heavy Brooklyn accent was making him sound worse than he was, which was pretty bad.

Wringing his hands together, Dulan says he will do anything to help, anything, just ask, anything, just keep the mad American away.

Dulan is given a script to read out as he phones Cho with his new information.

"All the Americans will be on the boat at 4:26 tomorrow afternoon, jetty two, getting ready to leave China; it's get them or lose them time."

Cho is delighted and plans a quick attack with all the surviving brood. Vivan wants the beating heart of the leader just as Cho takes his head. They plan to hit them at 4 pm just before they leave.

Using Jake's sniping skills, a kill zone is set up using the tall buildings around the ship's berth in jetty two. Willie and Jake set up in an old warehouse, John and Donald on top of an apartment block, while Duke and Norman Vincenti. (Former Philly gangland enforcer) set up in a boat three berths down with a clear shot at their own boat's bridge door.

Inside their boat are six manikins from an old clothes warehouse all posed to look like them from the outside to make the boat look occupied, music also plays from the interior radio and the ship's interior lights are set low to further bait the trap.

"Sniper one set, covering boarding ramp," Jake calmly sends.

"Sniper two set, covering the bridge door," Duke says.

"Sniper three set, covering rear walk space," calls John. "We wait." It was 3 pm.

At 3.50, a taxi pulls up and out gets Vivan, Cho and Vinux, all walk towards the boat, guns ready, all are armed with the Chinese version of an Uzi 9mm.

"Sniper one, no target."

"Sniper two, no target."

"Sniper three, no target. They should be coming into sight in 20 seconds."

The Koban slink along towards the boat. "I can see people inside," Vinux whispers.

"Sniper one, no target."

"Sniper two, no target."

"Sniper three, targets! I can see all three, can you guys scope my area?"

Two replies of 'can do if we relocate, but our areas will not be covered' fills his ears.

"Do it! I may be able to give us standing targets. I have a plan. Fire on my command."

Moments later. "We are in position, partial view of targets."

"Sniper one, same as two, partial view."

John gets on the phone he had used to contact Cho. "Hey, Cho, how are they hanging?"

The Koban spin around. Cho is holding the handset looking wildly about, standing stock still checking the area. All have the Uzis up ready to shoot.

"Sniper one, target the female," whispers John.

"Sniper two, target the guy wearing the blue jacket."

"I have Cho, FIRE!"

POW! POW! POW! Almost simultaneous reports crack across the water. Three Koban drop as if puppet strings were cut. All three die instantly.

"OOOOOOH, NICE! SCALEMITE, DID YOU SEE THE WAY THE HEADS JUST BLEW APART? LOOK, THERE ARE BIG LUMPS OF BRAINS ALL OVER THE DOCK. QUICK, GO GET SOME BEFORE ALL THOSE SCALE-DIPPED SEAGULLS WOLF IT ALL DOWN."

They quickly board their boat and cast off. Throttling up, they leave the harbour, six manikins floating in their wake.

It is a long journey back to the United States, three months pass.

In the States, President Erika Brynja/Flinexa has been busy.

White House Oval Office, Present Day

"Gather all our hatchmates. My time is near."

Erika Brynja/Flinexa leans on her desk, the large three pane bay window at her back and stretches her arms above her head.

"I can feel the change starting."

Thomas Drake, now secretary of defence, nods and backs out the door, calling to his secretary he says, "Phone the list under special VIPs, call me when everyone acknowledges."

"What about this one highlighted in green?" questions the secretary with a frown.

"Never mind that treacherous scale slime! She/It? can rot, just get the rest," growls Drake.

Thinking to herself, the secretary wonders what, as she reads down the list her finger following the lines of names, 'Orina' had done to warrant that outburst?

Orina was the black lizard of the family. Hatching late from a small egg, Orina should have died soon after hatching; he was a runt! Barely five feet, fully grown. On hatching, he was no bigger than a chicken, so could only take over small animals. His first was a weasel-like four-legged dinosaur, and that set the trend, he was a smart, shrewd, totally vicious little predator, his hatchmates hated him for being different; it did not help that he was as bent as a hairpin. He jumped ship just as one of the six boats passed through what's now the Greek islands as they headed towards the continent's mainland; he was not missed.

When humans eventually came onto the island the only host, he would fit into were small females, he liked it, and it gave him a sense of power.

Koban females were the dominant ones in the species and the only ones to be able to transform and leave the planet.

Orina fiercely wanted to be female, it may have been the isolation or the small egg, lack of oxygen, whatever. Orina was several sandwiches short of a picnic.

When his hatchmates finally come across him again by chance on the island, he is shunned as an abomination and left there to rot.

Orina swears revenge. 'Hell, hath no fury like a woman scorned.' As the men of Lemnos found out.

Orina had taken the form of a beautiful woman called 'Hypsipyle', killing her in the process. In this form, he wanders around the villages smiling and nodding to all, until the husband Atticus turns up.

Hypsipyle/Orina is dragged back to the villa and repeatedly raped. Totally unprepared for this with no knowledge of what was happening with the sex (the transfer of memories had not been fully successful). Hypsipyle/Orina thought it was a form of attack.

Atticus finished with his 'wife', threw Hypsipyle/Orina into the bedroom and leaves to drink with his friends.

Hypsipyle/Orina is cleaned up by neighbours and finds a disturbing truth. All the men on the island treat the women the same way. Every night! EVERY day! EVERY MONTH, EVERY GOD'S CURSED YEAR!

Hypsipyle/Orina tells them of a plan to stop the abuse. Humans sleep (silly things). The next night the women slaughter every man on the island as they sleep. (Later this would be woven into the *Jason and the Argonauts* tale.)

The women rule the island for years. Hypsipyle/Orina leaves when people start noticing her lack of aging; gathering all her possessions and money she heads along the coast to Spain. Vengeance in mind, she/he starts to track down her hatchmates.

White House Oval Office, Present Day

Silivan walks around the oval office reading from a data pad; she is the same height and build as Flinexa and will take charge when Flinexa departs. Reading from the pad, she says, "The tunnel is prepared and goes directly towards the central caldera, as you know, Yellowstone has three calderas in the super volcano, you will enter through 'Dragon Cave', which will be sealed after you are in the special chamber by a small shaped geological charge designed to bring down the tunnel walls. As you planned it, I will subsume the human double we surgically altered to look like you and take your place as president, keeping our control in America intact. With you safely sealed in the chamber, we wait for your dramatic departure. No doubt, results from the seismic sensors around the park will alert the secret service that an immediate eruption is forecast, this will of course start the evacuation protocol to abandon the White House. I will be taken to Air Force One along with all our hatchmates and flown to Hickam Field in Hawaii, well out of the danger area that will virtually destroy the United States' infrastructure, farming and manufacturing bases, covering most of it in six inches of ash according to our researchers. With myself being the president, I will govern America from Hawaii. Rebuilding the country. So many displaced people to process! Our rule of the food stock will remain intact." Silivan/President Erika Brynja (the second) smiles.

"Excellent! I leave the Earth Koban into your care, may your transition be soon, Silivan."

Flinexa opens her special drawer and hands her sister a wriggling naked rat, holding her own up in a toast, she says, "Cheers." Both rats disappear down extended throats.

Orina using various forms throughout the years, all female, tracks down and kills thirty-eight Koban males. Tracking the smaller groups that established in Europe and the United Kingdom, where she has resided for the last seventy odd years since the end of WW2, until word of Koban in America reaches 'her' ears.

Boarding a transatlantic cruise ship, Orina is in the form of a petite English woman called Vivian Smythe and is heading to New York to start 'her' cull in America for the first time. The end game is near.

New York, Hell's Kitchen

"Good to be home, boss, I can tell ya." Big Duke has an ear-to-ear grin.

They were all sitting in Murphy's Bar on 14th Street; it had become a headquarters of a sort as they planned out what to do next.

"Has Tom Marks uncovered any news on what's happening?" asks Norman Vincenti, the ex-Philly hitman and ex-Dulce inmate from his seat by the bar.

"OOO yeah, he has some wild stories and will be over later to fill us in," says John/Zin.

Willie and Jake are playing cards one table down. Two half-finished beers and one empty are beside them on the table. Donald Firemaker walks back from the toilet and nods to them as he sits by his cards, which are spread out in front of his seat.

"Don't go to the john for the next five minutes, guys." The big Apache laughs.

Good-natured groans from his card mates. Firemaker was notorious for leaving toxic messages every now and again.

The doors open and in slinks Tom Marks; he heads towards John/Zin.

"CHRIST, WHAT'S THAT SMELL?" Everybody nods towards Donald, who stands and gives a bow from the waist, farting at the same time…Class.

Tom Marks had been a busy man; he had surveillance photos; he had taped together shredded White House stationary; he had witness statements albeit from kooks and crazies, but it all made sense in a way, especially to John and Ohna.

The shredded White House paper was a map of Yellowstone Park showing the entrance to Dragon Cave and an estimated date of departure, but no arrival point. The date of departure was two weeks away.

One other piece from the National Enquirer's flashy headline stated: 'Woman on Cruise Ship Turns into Dinosaur and Eats a Hamster'.

"WE HAVE A NEW PLAYER, SCALEMITE, BUT WHERE DID THE NEW FEMALE COME FROM? WE KNOW THERE SHOULD ONLY BE TWO LEFT NOW WE'VE DEALT WITH THE CHINESE CLUTCH."

"Don't know, Ohna, we need to find out wha—"

"That won't be a problem! One of my guys followed her off the boat, she is a very pretty tiny little thing," butts in Marks with his annoying nasal voice.

"TINY, TINY, you sure?" John and Ohna say at the same time.

"HE IS STILL ALIVE, SCALE SCRUBBER! THAT CHANGES THINGS!"

"Of course, I am sure!" Marks says with a sniff of his nose, which he looks down it at John. "She is here in New York."

"WE MIGHT GET THE SCALE-MUDDLED CREATURE TO HELP, OR AT LEAST SET THE MAD SCALE TICK ON HIS HATCHMATES."

"Where is she staying, Tom?" questions John.

"The Marriot in Times Square, fifteen thirty-five Broadway, corner of forty-fifth Street," rattles off Marks.

"Thanks for all the help; we will keep you in the loop." John nods farewell to Marks who slinks back out the door. He then turns to the others. "We need to catch a snake. Phone a cab, let's go see the 'lady'."

They all get in the cab and cut across to Times Square, a fifty buck 'tip' to the bellboy and the room number for the small English woman is gleaned.

"Okay, everyone knows what's what: being small she will be fairly weak, but we take no chances. SET PHASERS ON STUN (he had always wanted to say that), I mean tasers to stun." John/Zin grins.

With a gentle knock on the door of Room 527 in the Marriot and a quiet call of 'Room Service', they wait for the door to open. As soon as the door moves, Big Duke ploughs into the room, a very feminine shriek fills the space. Vivian Smythe is overpowered and strapped to a chair with duct tape.

"MY TURN, SCALEMITE." Ohna shimmers into view. The guys have seen Ohna before but it still blows them away, every time.

"HELLO, SCALE MOULD, HOW HAVE YOU BEEN? NICE DRESS, BY THE WAY. WE MAY BE AFTER THE SAME THING. WE THINK FLINEXA IS READY TO BE A MOTHER, I HAVE BEEN PICKING UP RISING GRAVITOX READINGS SINCE YESTERDAY."

"You must be the ParVon (Hunters) I have heard about for such a long time, you look rather fetching, my dear, simply stunning. Your companion is rather coarse though, don't you think?" said Vivian with a posh English upper-class lilt.

"Let's cut the crap, Koban, we don't have time, if she is going to use the super volcano in Yellowstone, we are all in danger…You too 'Princess'," growls John/Zin.

"I see." Crossing shapely but short legs, she says, "Do tell, what do you have in mind, dear chap."

Blackhawk Helicopter Over Yellowstone Park

Ten black-clad Special Forces soldiers rope drop from the chopper and take up defensive positions around the entrance to Dragons Cave. Capt. Russel Gunnison waves a strobe light to signal the Sikorsky CH53 King Stallion heavy lift helicopter to land.

Unseen by no one other than her fellow hatchmates, a now huge forty-five feet snakelike bodied Flinexa is helped down deep into the cave. Settled in the chamber dug for this purpose, Flinexa starts to form her super hard shell. This will take several days. The tunnel is collapsed sealing her in. All the Koban leave with the Sikorsky. The Special Forces Marines think it was an exercise and know nothing different. The time for Flinexa to leave is a matter of days away.

Murphy's Bar, Hell's Kitchen

Big Duke calls over to the barman, "Hey, Louie, turn up the TV, wills ya?"

'FURTHER TO OUR STORY, WORRYING REPORTS ARE COMING OUT OF YELLOWSTONE PARK, SEISMIC ACTIVITY AND MASSIVE BURSTS OF STEAM HAVE VULCANOLOGISTS VERY WORRIED.'

"Watcha think, boss, this your Koban maybe?" Duke calls over to John.

"Could be, Duke, you getting anything, Ohna?"

"SCALEMITE, THESE READINGS CAN'T BE RIGHT! I JUST STARTED TO PICK IT UP. THE BUILD UP OF GRAVITOX PULSES ARE WAY LARGER THAN THE MOUNT SAINT HELENS ONE. THIS IS A LARGE FEMALE, THAT'S FOR SURE."

"We need to get to Yellowstone and stop this."

The TV is still playing away when they hear:

VULCANOLOGISTS HAVE DECLARED AN EMERGENCY EVACUATION OF YELLOWSTONE PARK AND GIVEN WARNING OF THE IMMINENT ERUPTION OF THE YELLOWSTONE VOLCANO. THE WHITE HOUSE HAD THIS TO SAY. The picture cuts to the White House situation room.

A STATE OF EMERGENCY HAS BEEN ACTIVATED FOR THE YELLOWSTONE AREA. MILITARY LAW HAS BEEN GRANTED. AN ORDERLY EVACUATION OF THE SURROUNDING AREA IS MANDATORY. ALL ROADS WILL HAVE ONE WAY TRAFFIC ONLY LEADING TO SAFE ZONES. WE URGE YOU NOT TO PANIC OR HORDE FOODSTUFFS AND WATER. THIS WILL BE SUPPLIED ON SITE. FURTHER NEWS WILL BE GIVEN AS IT ARISES.

The six comrades stare open mouthed at the screen. "What the fuck! Phone Vivian Smythe, tell 'Her' to get over here." John points to Vincenti and says, "Norm, you go pick up Tom Marks, don't take any shit, get him here fast."

With no way of now getting to Yellowstone Park, John is unsure what to do, so he wants as many heads looking at this as possible.

"YOU WILL NEED TO LOG THIS, SCALEMITE, SEND AN EARLY REPORT EVEN THOUGH NO ONE WILL ANSWER."

"I will do that soon, Ohna, let's have some ideas first." John looks over as the door opens and in goose-stepped a pale Tom Marks.

"Here he is, boss." Vincenti's big hand is resting on his shoulder.

A stuttering nasal whine from Marks drifts across the room.

"Unhand me, you thug, what's the meaning of this outrage?" At this, in strides Vivian Smythe walking like a super model.

"And who is this charming, gentleman, may I ask?" It is love at first sight; Marks may actually get to meet a real reptilian.

"Vivian Smythe, this is Tom Marks. Tom, this is Vivian. By the way, Vivian, Tom is investigating the chance that reptilians are really running the White House, he has written a vast amount of literature on the subject." John winks.

"OOOOOH! That was you! I luuuuuuved reading about that, you must tell me aaaall about it," breathes Vivian batting her perfectly made up eyes at him.

The planning session quickly comes to the conclusion that Flinexa will leave Earth, there is no way of stopping her, survival planning comes next and what to do about the remaining Koban on Earth. Obviously, they will have planned to be well away before the volcano erupts, how and when are discussed. Norman Vincenti clears his throat and makes a shame-faced confession.

"Guys, I tried to kill the last president a few years back."

Every head turns towards him, Big Duke gives him a professional nod of respect.

"We planned it to be done during a disaster we would rig up; this would set the security protocols for the president to be evacuated and flown out on Air Force One. I was going to put a stinger missile into it, killing the man by taking out the plane. I still have the stinger in a lockup outside the airport," Vincenti says with a nod.

"That will still work! They are bound to get the White House staff to safety before the volcano erupts, we can have someone waiting with the missile," John says.

"I will do that! I want to destroy the last of my hatchmates; I want revenge for what they did to me over the years, please let me do it, you can then do what you like with me after that," pleads Vivian.

"And I will help the dear lady do just that," says Tom with a nod.

Norman Vincenti gives the lovestruck pair directions to where the stinger is stored and quick instructions on how to use it; the pair head out to get it and wait for the White House evacuation, whenever that occurs. John heads back to his apartment to log in his report.

"ParVon Zin calling in, we have failed to stop a large Koban female from leaving TXP73-S3. We a—"

"SCALEMITE, I AM PICKING UP A SCOUT SHIP! THEY HAVE FOUND US! THEY ARE TRYING TO TALK BUT WE ARE NOT RECEIVING."

"WOW, AFTER ALL THIS TIME! Tell them the co-ordinates of the volcano, they may be able to sense the Koban and deal with it from orbit," gushes John/Zin.

"THEY HAVE MUCH BETTER SCANNERS NOW IT SEEMS AND HAVE LOCKED ONTO THE KOBAN MOTHER BUT WILL NEED TIME TO GET TO A LOWER ORBIT, WHICH WILL BE DANGEROUS BECAUSE OF ALL THE METALLIC JUNK THAT IS WHIZZING AROUND THE PLANET FROM THE EARTHLINGS' SPACE EXPLORATION, THEY ESTIMATE ONE CYCLE."

At that same time, the TV station reports the immediate evacuation of the White House staff to Hawaii in order to be able to co-ordinate the response regarding the impending volcanic explosion.

Vivian and Tom get a phone call to warn them that the evacuation is almost underway, they ready the missile and head for Andrews Airforce Base in Maryland. Parking in the Flower Village Mobile Home Park, they wait for Marine One and a trailing convoy of helicopters to deliver the president and her staff to Air Force One, all the staff and crew are thralls, slaves with no choice but to obey.

They don't have long to wait and nearly miss the big plane's take off.

It is well within range of the stinger as Vivian hears the steady beep of the lock-on get faster as a lock is confirmed.

A quick pull of the trigger and whooosh! It's done.

There is a flash on the starboard wing as the missile hits the engine, the big plane leans over and spirals down into the ground, just missing the Stephan Decatur Middle School before ploughing into Pinewood Park, totally destroying the plane and killing all on board.

The Randorian scout ship is now clear of the debris field and is in low orbit over Yellowstone Park. Advances in Randorian science and physics had been slow but one development was an 'Anti-Matter Dart'. The anti-matter held in check by a magnetic containment unit (the dart) until it hits a specific genetic marker, in this case Koban.

The dart is fired by the scout ship's rail gun and strikes the Earth at high velocity, piercing it all the way to Koban's ultra-hard shell. The anti-matter strikes normal matter and both explosively cancel each other out. Flinexa no longer exists.

'BREAKING NEWS! VOLCANOLOGISTS STUDYING THE YELLOWSTONE VOLCANIC DISTURBANCE HAVE ANNOUNCED THAT THE

READINGS AND SEISMIC REPORTS HAVE ALL RETURNED TO A STABLE LEVEL. NO CONCLUSIONS TO WHY THE VOLCANIC DISTURBANCE OCCURRED IN THE FIRST PLACE CAN BE FOUND. VOLCANOLOGISTS ARE PUZZLED.'

Cheers erupt from the small group in Murphy's Bar. Ohna receives co-ordinates from the scout ship for a clandestine pickup. ParVon Zin will meet fellow Randorians for the first time in over sixty-five million cycles; he is, as might be expected, rather nervous.

The pickup point is in Prospect Park, just beside the lake and set for 3 am the next day; it goes off without a hitch.

Dark Side of Earth's Moon, Same Day

ParVon Zin stands at attention, tail straight, eyes front. The tall female commander says, "Relax, Zin, after all this time, I have no idea what rank you hold, if any? We have been receiving your reports for hundreds of cycles but never got a reply to hails, so we were sent out to investigate this weird world you described. Do they really go dormant for long periods of time? Unbelievable, our conquest of this world will be even easier."

"WHAT! NO, YOU CAN'T DO THAT!" cries a shocked Zin.

Zin is now able to contact Randor (The planet has been re-inhabited for millennia now). He pleads his case for the humans.

Zin tells them of the advancements the humans have made since the dawn of time; he admits to helping along the way a little and admits the Koban did the same thing. Gunpowder in China for example, Romans' use of concrete, Viking boat building designs. All assisted with ideas from the shapeshifters.

Zin's final plea is for the humans to be formally approached by the Federation of Aligned Planets to join and act as a full member. Being way out on the spiral arm of the Galaxy Earth is so removed from mainstream Galactic life it would make little difference to humanity one way or the other, only the Koban (drifting) or the Randorians Stardrive had the capacity to travel the distances required to reach Earth. Zin states that Earth could be used as a staging area to cover this section of space, keeping an eye out for Koban incursions this far out. It is agreed that an ambassador would contact the humans and start talks towards mutual protection and trade treaties being drawn up. One quick item the Randorians noticed straightaway was the abundance of Helium-3 on the Earth's Moon, this alone as a refuelling point would guarantee Earth's acceptance into the federation.

Take Me to Your Leaders

A message was sent to every country on Earth. The scout ship now decloaked was visible on every sensor Earth had pointing out into space, mass panic ensues! Until after repeated pleas from the Randorians with TV film and very slick marketing is starting to gain some trust.

A meeting of Randorians and Earth leaders is arranged in the UN building for the next day. Having already explained their ability to shapeshift, the offer is made to appear as human. This is taken under advisement and will be given closer to the agreed time.

The Randorians have sent video of themselves so everyone on earth knows what they look like. Scary eight feet tall dinosaurs! With teeth!

Thank you, Steven Spielberg! And every other non-scary ET-type film that was out there, it was that that won people over.

It was also let known that Zin had been on the planet for some time (they kept it to a couple of centuries) and his exploits with the native Hopi could be verified and put into a good light showing him as a stranded voyager playing nice with the natives.

Spotted Elk was flown into Washington to tell of his adopted son's exploits; it was all a very slick PR exercise and was working well.

Zin's appearance in the UN building finished it off; he spoke for three hours answering questions before introducing Ohna, who has been told what to say about the time they had been here for. Ohna's avatar pops into view.

PANDEMONIUM! GASPS AND CRIES OF FEAR, ASTONISHMENT AND JOY ALL IN EQUAL MEASURE.

"HELLO, TERANS, MY SCALEMITE HAS SPOKEN THE TRUTH AND SEEING ME (giving a graceful twirl) WILL LET YOU SEE HOW WE REALLY LOOK. MY BEST FRIENDS HAVE ALL BEEN TERANS SINCE OUR CREW WERE KILLED IN THE CRASH OVER TWO HUNDRED YEARS AGO. WE HAVE COME TO LOVE LIVING HERE AND BEING WITH YOU AND WITH YOUR PERMISSION, STAY AND JOIN WITH YOU IN A NEW AND LASTING PARTNERSHIP."

With a graceful bow, Ohna walks over and stands by her mate's side, scales gleaming in the overhead spotlights.

The video of this is streamed worldwide. Ohna is a huge success, especially with the younger computer game-playing audience, where Ohna slightly resembles a character in the computer game 'SpaceRaptor 3'.

This goes on for weeks, John and Ohna are now the faces of the Randorian contact team. Team leader Atinas and her executive officer Tabuu have been down several times, a hyper-radio comms unit has been set up in the UN and full contact is established with Randor.

Trade and mutual defence treaties are drawn up, and an embassy is constructed on Hopi Reservation land at the request of John Running Fox/Zin.

As he has now been given the temporary title of Randorian Earth ambassador, John hires his own security people who all willingly agree to join up. Donald Firemaker, Duke Geneva, Norman Vincenti, Willie Hawkins and Jake Lincon. The opening of the new Randorian Embassy is a spectacle you would not believe.

With the landed scout ship as a backdrop and the six Randorian crew partying large along with John's friends, world leaders, invited guests and a mass of news people. The only ones missing were two lovebirds who could at that time have cared less; Vivian and Tom were enjoying each other on a remote island getaway in the South Seas (the Randorians would have picked up Vivian's Koban scent in a heartbeat).

The party lasted three days, the non-sleeping Randorians not stopping for anything, other than to watch fascinated as the humans fell asleep.

It was hilarious to watch 8 ft reptiles dance in front of sleeping humans, waving arms before faces and sticking their tongues out, very advanced for a space faring species. LOL.

A couple of thousand miles away in a tasteful waterside beach house, Vivian Smythe lies naked on the king size bed, the white silk sheets silhouetting her breast, one arm bent at the elbow, a sculpted chin resting on a delicate hand with perfectly manicured and painted nails waiting patiently for Tom Marks to stop spluttering and coughing after blurting out, "WHAT!"

Delicate painted lips repeated, "You know I am a guy, right?" Peals of delicate laughter can be heard down the beach. Who said shapeshifters had no sense of humour?

Glossary

ANUNNAKI. Bird like reptilians with a bird's head vestigial wings and powerful body. They are slavers and lust for gold. Not a part of the Alliance of planets, their arrogance forbids it.

BELATANS. Squat Iguana like bipedal reptilians. Bankers and Lawyers, all Alliance business is done through Belatan. Enormously powerful beings as they hold most of the secrets of each race. Ruthless when it comes to money or law.

BOLDONIANS. Most humanoid looking of the reptilians, merchants supplying the Alliance with everything sellable, gentle beings until business is threatened, then they declare war until it is resolved, they have a vast armada of merchant ships, heavily armed merchant ships.

ENDINEKI. Scientists, Engineers, and Medical Specialists. Looking like bi-pedal Geckos. The entire planet is focused on these disciplines. Highly sought after as healers and teachers.

HUMANS. Non-shape shifting beings. Genetically altered by the Gishma tribe of the Anunnaki to be a slave species and to work the gold mines on Thera Three (Earth). Or as the Anunnaki named them when they created what is now modern man. Adamu.

KOBAN. Only true parasitic shape shifter, snake like on hatching it must subsume a host to survive and grow.

POLTOX. Alligators on legs, extremely aggressive species, they hire out to any species as security guards and mercenaries, very loose ties to the Alliance.

RANDORIANS. Oldest of the reptilians, and developers of the Star Drive system, thought to be do-gooders by some. The Randorians are the main component of the Koban hunting teams.

SILVENEXIANS. Insectoid race with three separate species, Red, Blue, and Black, secretive, and sly the reptilians do not trust them.

THIBRANS. Smallest of the reptilians, with a large round head atop a spindly body, barely five feet high, timid, and cowardly. They were totally subjugated by the Anistol Anunnaki eons ago and made into their slaves. They are the Anunnaki's servants, doing whatever is required by their overlords and masters.

Ingram Content Group UK Ltd.
Milton Keynes UK
UKHW020115300523
422450UK00008B/75